A FIRE SO WILD

A FIRE SO WILD

a novel

Sarah Ruiz-Grossman

HARPER

An Imprint of HarperCollins*Publishers*

HarperCollins books may be purchased for educational, business, or sales promotional use. For information, please email the Special Markets Department at SPsales@harpercollins.com.

FIRST EDITION

Designed by Elina Cohen
Art throughout courtesy of Shutterstock / Lorthois Yuliya

Library of Congress Cataloging-in-Publication Data has been applied for.

ISBN 978-0-06-330542-7

23 24 25 26 27 LBC 5 4 3 2 1

To the survivors who shared their stories with me
at the worst possible time in their lives,

thank you.

A FIRE SO WILD

PROLOGUE

She stared at the house, engulfed in flames. The tall, alternately white and bright orange spikes were licking at all of their memories, devouring them. Cheeks singed, eyes narrowed and swimming with tears, she searched the façade until, finally, she found what she was looking for, what she'd feared: on the second floor, a dark shape stood in the window. She screamed then, her whole body contorting with the effort, her throat scalded. Her cries were swallowed by the deafening cracking of wood, the whining of the house's foundations as it threatened to collapse.

They hadn't all gotten out.

PART I

water

AUGUST

The surface of Lake Anza was so still that it reflected the surrounding trees in a perfect mirror image, the sky captured cloud by cloud, the entire world in this body of water. This was Abigail's favorite time of day: just after the crack of dawn, when the woods were quiet but for the chirps of waking birds and insects, when no one expected her to be anywhere at all. She stepped in, her body seizing as the cold enveloped her feet. Before she could change her mind, she dove, her hands, breasts, stomach, and legs slipping into the crisp water, each one of her skin cells coming alive. The shock was a welcome sensation. Too much of her life was spent feeling comfortable, she thought.

She would be turning fifty soon, and it hadn't escaped her that in all likelihood, more than half of her life was now behind her. Her body certainly didn't let her forget it. First, there were the hot flashes, which started last year and had only grown more intense over the hot, sticky summer nights. Then the sudden bouts of insomnia, which left her roaming the house before dawn, like a bear who'd wandered in by mistake: a little stunned, surprisingly hungry, mostly frustrated at not being able to find a comfortable position, even in her own bed. But it was the dryness that really caught her off guard—nothing a little lube couldn't fix, but still, she wondered why women didn't warn one another about such things. A heads-up might have kept her from scrolling manically through WebMD at one a.m., after a frustrating tussle with Taylor, to whom she had insisted that yes, she was turned on; yes, it was good for her; no, she didn't know what the hell was going on, maybe it was stress—the usual culprit. A few impatient clicks and frustrated scrolls later, Abigail made the gratifying discovery that it was, in fact, yet another symptom of menopause. She also came across the unfortunate descriptor that her vagina was "atrophying." When she Googled that, in turn, two definitions popped up: 1. to waste away; and 2. a gradual decline in effectiveness or vigor. Synonyms: "shrivel," "wither," "decay," "wilt." Mazel tov.

Abigail slowed her strokes, which had grown messy and fitful with her thoughts. She ducked her head underwater, felt the whoosh of a watery silence surrounding her. She opened her eyes. Even with her goggles on, she couldn't see farther out than her hands, the murky waters rendered green by years of drought. She buried her feet into the warm mud of the lake's bottom. Something solid, to keep her still. She popped her head back above the surface and took in the ring that ran around the lake's edge, marking the spot where the water used to come up to, back before the rains stopped. The chalky rocks, wild tree roots, and long grass that used to be hidden beneath the line of the water were all visible now. They looked naked, exposed, like they hadn't asked for any of this.

Fifty was the year Abigail had spent her whole life measuring herself up against. When she thought of who she wanted to be, what she wanted to accomplish, she'd used the refrain: "I don't want to wake up at fifty and . . ." Now here she was, a couple months shy of the fated birthday, and when she took stock of it all, she wasn't sure she liked what she saw.

She'd had grand visions for her life. An overeager law school student, she'd pictured herself as a fighter for justice, the next Ruth Bader Ginsburg. Instead, she now spent her days in the confines of a small office, drafting proposals for grants from foundations that had far too much money and even more causes competing for it. On good days, she was proud of her job. "I work in affordable housing," she'd drop at one of the charity benefits Berkeley High parents organized each year. People oohed and aahed. So important. Yes, especially with the homeless problem around here, it's really getting to be out of hand, yes, yes, such critical work.

But on most days, Abigail saw her job for what it really was: paper pushing against the behemoths of capitalism and Big Tech, a battle long lost. For every affordable unit built, another ten multimillion-dollar homes and luxury condos went up. One step forward, one hundred back.

Just days ago, she'd gotten word that a project she'd been working on for months—a building going up on the city's west side, which she was trying to convert to mixed-income housing—was falling apart. She'd negotiated a unique partnership between the corporate developer, who'd built it; the city, who'd granted the land; and a local food bank, who could help identify reliable, low-income tenants. If the project succeeded, it would be the first of its kind in Berkeley, a successful public-private-nonprofit collaboration for housing (which was the kind of thing foundations absolutely ate up)—and it was Abigail's brainchild. In time, it could be replicated elsewhere, make a serious dent in the housing crisis statewide. But then, at the last minute, the developer pulled out. They said they couldn't possibly set aside a third of the apartments for low-income renters. They just couldn't get the budget to add up. (Their profits wouldn't be astronomical enough, they meant.) Maybe, just maybe, they could make 5 percent work. In a twenty-unit building, that meant one apartment. Just one, to be priced below market. And with that, Abigail's hopes and dreams had withered into dust. So much for making a difference. Making her mark. Making something of herself.

So on days like this, at the tail end of summer, when Abigail had a moment to step out of her routine and look at the big picture, she wondered if it was enough, really. What her life added up to.

Abigail stopped swimming, feeling her heart racing. She waded back toward shore, the insides of her thighs chafing against each other as she heard her mother's voice ringing in her head: *Make something of yourself, Abby.* It was a refrain her mother had repeated for as long as she could remember. The trouble was, Abigail wasn't entirely sure what she meant.

She picked up her towel, shaking the sand off and burying her face in the soft cotton, letting the darkness engulf her momentarily. Then she dragged the towel aggressively up each of her arms and down her legs. "Make something of yourself."

Did her son, Xavier, count? He was a senior at Berkeley High, a gem of a human. Even if the planet was overpopulated, the warming climate precipitating humanity toward a cycle of fires and floods of biblical proportions, certainly it was a net positive that she'd brought someone like Xavier into the world—so well educated, so thoughtful. He'd go on to do a lot of good one day, probably.

Abigail walked toward her car, rubbing her eye sockets and pinching the place on the bridge of her nose where her goggles had pressed in too hard. She had a good life, for fuck's sake. Who was her mother, anyway, to decide whether she had "made something of herself"? The woman lived alone in the same brownstone in Brooklyn where Abigail grew up, four stories of empty rooms, with only her weekly shabbat dinners at the rabbi's to look forward to.

"Make something of myself," Abigail muttered, turning on the car with an impatient flick of her wrist. She drove out of Tilden Park, her tires kicking up clouds of dust, tossing pebbles like tiny missiles to the feet of the tall redwood trees.

A few blocks downhill, Abigail pulled into her driveway. She took in her three-story, chestnut-shingled house, the thin slice of their deck's breathtaking view just visible from the street. Regal, deep green pines surrounded the deck then plunged down toward the miles of houses below, stretching all the way out to the bay.

If this wasn't a successful life, she didn't know what was. (Never mind that it was Taylor's earnings that had gotten them this house in the first place—an anxious thought for another day.)

Abigail turned the car off and paused with her hand on the door latch, knowing what awaited her inside: Taylor's silences, grown longer and heavier in recent months, and Xavier's adolescent moodiness, intensifying as senior year approached. She took her hand off the door and cranked her seat back, turning the radio to NPR. She closed her eyes. Just a little while longer in the quiet.

Suddenly, her eyes popped open. She knew what she would do. Yes. She'd throw a party. A fundraiser. She'd ask her friend Marcia to host. She had a fabulous house in the hills, with plenty of space and a view to die for. Abigail could invite all her friends, the whole network of Berkeley High parents. If done right, it would only take one night to raise the money they needed to make the deal work, to subsidize the remaining apartments for low-income renters. Her organization would be thrilled. And God knew, Berkeley High parents loved an excuse to throw their money at a problem, to sleep a little sounder at night.

She'd do it on her fiftieth birthday weekend. It was still a couple months away—plenty of time to plan. That way no one could refuse her. (Taylor couldn't very well be withdrawn, nor Xavier moody, at her birthday party.) She'd invite her mother to come from New York. She'd see just how well surrounded Abigail was, how full her life.

One had to celebrate things. Otherwise, what was life but a slow, mundane crawl toward an unavoidable end?

———

Right on the shoreline, where the edge of Berkeley melted into the water and the snowy egrets stood on long black legs in the shallows, where the highway's exhaust fumes dissipated into the bay, Sunny was tossing and turning in the back of the van, waking from a fitful sleep. It was hard to keep his eyes shut, feeling the moisture gathering between his thighs, the heat pressing into his chest, a slow smothering. He needed to get these windows open.

He wriggled one arm gingerly out from under Willow's head and pulled the other from under Aso, whose long, furry body emanated heat like a sixty-pound furnace. Crawling up between the two front seats, Sunny winced as he turned the key, started the engine, and sent the old vehicle rumbling to life. He peeked back over his shoulder. Willow pulled a pillow over her head and groaned, willing the noise away. Sunny cranked the driver's-side window open, inhaling a sliver of morning breeze rolling in off the water. This was his favorite place to park: on West Frontage Road, just on the other side of the highway, along a semi-forgotten strip of beaches—if you could even call the ten-foot-wide patches of mud and rocky sand that. To Sunny, it was a holy respite from long days working construction under the punishing California sun. His own private peace.

He glanced at the time blinking on the dashboard: 9:14 a.m. Shit. He was going to be late. Again.

"Willow," he said, crawling back over to the mattress in the back of the van. She didn't budge. He dug through his gym bag squeezed up against the side door, lifting out one shirt after another and holding them up to his nose. None were clean. He took another quick whiff to find the least-rank one and slipped it on over his head. By noon, most of the guys would be sweating to high heaven anyhow.

"Willow, baby," he said, louder. He didn't like to wake her, knowing how her insomnia kept her up at night.

Willow shoved the pillow from her face and squinted her sleep-crusted eyes. "What is it?"

Sunny leaned over her. "Babe, you're gonna have to walk and feed Aso. I have to get to the site before they fire me for real this time. You okay to handle him?"

"Of course I am, you fretter. Get out of here." Willow pulled Sunny in for a kiss and then shoved him away. "We'll be fine, won't we, bud?" The old pit bull padded over to Willow's outstretched arms and sat squarely on her stomach, eliciting a humph and a giggle.

Sunny paused for a moment to take it in—his two most precious beings, all cozied up.

Then he turned to leave, crawling toward the van's back door, throwing it open. As he hopped down to the cement, he looked out over the bay. The shimmering blue water extended before him, meeting the dark, jagged mountains of Marin to one side and buoying dozens of shipping containers along the South Bay to the other. Square in the middle rolled San Francisco's hills, dotted with tiny white and beige houses. The gray towers crowded into the city's downtown sent a pang into Sunny's stomach. He flashed back to the first months he'd spent there, over a decade ago, on his own for the first time, a nineteen-year-old in the cold, fog-swept city. He slept in bus stops and under bridges, hell-bent on not going back to his parents' in Los Angeles. On the upside, that was where he'd met Willow.

Sunny finished tying the laces on his work boots and gave one last peek into the van. Aso and Willow were a pile of limbs, already asleep again. He softly shut the van doors. Jogging at a modest clip, he could get to the job site by ten a.m. He'd be an hour late, but it was nothing his supervisor couldn't let slide. He'd gotten away with worse before—not showing up at all some days, when Willow had one of her episodes and try as he might, Sunny couldn't get her to rise from bed, or even muster the will to eat. When she was like that, Sunny didn't leave her side. Not after the one time he had and he'd come back to find her . . . He didn't like to think about it.

Jogging up University Avenue, past the rush of commuter cars and caffeine-desperate workers waiting in line outside cafes, Sunny spotted from afar the new high-rise being built on the west side. Its windows glistened in the morning sun, a golden promise.

Months ago, Jo from the food bank had suggested he and Willow apply for a place there. Apparently, the building was willing to rent out some apartments at affordable rates, if the tenants came recommended. Willow filled out an application, and Jo said they'd hear back soon. Sunny played along, not believing for a second that they'd get it. That's not how things usually worked out for them.

But he had to admit, eyeing the building shooting up toward the sky, hugging the edge of the bay, the idea thrilled him. Their own place. Finally. A bed to stretch out in. A bathroom with a shower. Some privacy. Some quiet. A safe, stable place for Willow to get back on her feet.

Sunny didn't believe in God; no higher power he trusted would allow what they'd been through. Still, he prayed. Silently, barely even admitting to himself that that's what he was doing. He prayed they'd get the apartment. Some ease. A chance at something better.

He fiddled with the locket hanging from a chain around his neck. When he pushed it in at the sides, it clicked open to two tiny pictures: one of him and his mom, when he was about five years old, backdropped by a fake, cloud-filled sky from a strip mall photo booth in downtown LA; and one of Willow, her mouth cracked open wide, midlaugh, from the days after they'd first met. They were two young runaways with no family, no home, no money—just an instant connection and the same magnetic pull to dream. If he had known then all the ways life would conspire to fuck with them, would he have kissed her as they climbed to the peak of Mount Sutro to gaze at the full moon? Would he have married her in a makeshift ceremony on China Beach, Aso as their only witness, shivering in the wind, exchanging lockets and swearing to each other: "It's us against the world"? Hell yeah, he would.

After he got to work (apologizing half-heartedly to his boss, who underpaid him because he was still part-time and not a member of the union), Sunny watched the cement pour out of the mixer, lulled by its slow oozing into the foundation of the new house. He cursed himself for forgetting to bring a second

T-shirt to soak in cold water and throw over his neck. The afternoon was turning into the kind of hot that made his skin feel like it was sizzling, the beating sun penetrating his pores, every drop of sweat instantly evaporating and leaving him coated in a thin crust of salt. As he moved over to lift a long, wooden plank, balancing it over his shoulder to carry it into the backyard, Sunny felt like his limbs were moving through molasses, the air thick with the weight of the sun's rays. Tossing the heavy beam to the ground, Sunny wiped his brow and looked at the partially built house.

It would stick out like a sore thumb in this neighborhood. The modern, sleek black paneling made for an uncanny contrast to the older, shingled homes surrounding it, with triangle roofs and wild yards. Sunny knew most of the new houses were being built like this, rectangles with sharp edges and glass panes. No more rounded window nooks or built-in bookshelves. It made him sad for a reason he couldn't quite put his finger on. He wondered if the new owners would get curtains to block passersby from gazing into their house through the floor-to-ceiling windows, or if that was the point.

As he walked around the edge of the freshly painted pool, empty of water, Sunny imagined the future residents filling it to the brim despite the drought. They would dive in headfirst and swim lazy laps before settling at one end, sipping on a cold drink. He wondered if they'd pause for a moment then, feeling the refreshing tang of lemonade fizzling on the backs of their tongues, listening to the chorus of jays in the surrounding elms. If they'd think about the workers whose sweat had dripped into the slats of their wood floors, whose skin cells were embedded in their windowsills.

———

In the heart of the city, around the corner from Martin Luther King Jr. Civic Center Park, where a drum circle met on Thursdays and the farmers' market on Saturdays, inside the massive, stark white building of Berkeley High, Mar walked down the hallway thinking that this school was both not as bad and worse than she had imagined. Not as bad because the twelfth-grade classes weren't, as she'd feared, any harder than the junior-year ones at her old school in San Jose, nor did her classmates appear to be any smarter. But also worse, because Mar somehow hadn't anticipated just how much it would suck to be the new girl in her last year of high school.

At her old school, Mar felt like herself: confident, walking around in giggling, arm-linked packs with her friends, boldly challenging teachers in the classroom. Here, she was a ghost of herself. Other students called out one another's names in the halls, collided in dramatic hugs and fist bumps after summer break, and Mar floated through them, showing up late to class because she couldn't find the room, eating lunch in the park to avoid being the loser sitting alone in the cafeteria. How quickly her sense of self evaporated when the people who'd always known her weren't around.

Mar ducked into the bathroom, which was mercifully empty, and pulled out her phone. She considered calling her mom, telling her that this was all a terrible mistake—she shouldn't have moved to her dad's in Berkeley, she should just come back to San Jose, where she'd grown up and they'd all been happy all those years ago, before her dad fucked up and her parents split. But she also knew how hard her dad had fought to get her here, how he'd spent over a year on a waitlist for rare affordable housing in North Berkeley, just so she could attend the prestigious local public high school he taught at, so she could spend her senior year there, in time for college applications.

Mar tucked her phone back into her pocket with a determined shove. She was going to make herself some friends, goddamn it. It couldn't be that hard.

She marched across the hall into the office of the dean of student life. After waiting impatiently for the bored administrator behind the desk to lift his eyes to meet hers, Mar asked for their list of clubs. The gray-haired man arched his bushy eyebrows and wordlessly pushed a stack of pamphlets across his desk. Mar smiled tightly and tucked them under her arm, moving to sit in a chair in the corner of the office. She splayed them out in her lap and set aside basketball, soccer, and softball. The only cardio she did voluntarily was dancing. She flipped more slowly through the leaflets for debate club and the school paper—much more her vibe. But it was a bright green pamphlet that caught her eye, slipped between the theater club brochure and one for competitive knitters: birdwatching.

Ever since Mar was little, she had always felt freest outdoors. Back when her family was still whole, Mar and her parents would drive down to Santa Cruz on weekends. They'd lie side by side on their matching striped towels, each holding a book strategically positioned above their head to block the sun while they read. Mar and her mom would eventually get up to wade at the edge of the ocean, never swimming—the Pacific was way too cold for that—but letting the tide dig their feet into warm puddles. When the sun set, the sandpipers would come out. The small brown-and-white birds descended onto the water's edge, marching together by the dozens in their pitter-patter way, scurrying along the damp shoreline, rushing away as the waves came in. Mar was always mesmerized by their synchronized movements, by the assuredness of their unity.

Birdwatching it was, then.

The next day, she stood outside the classroom door and felt

her armpits break out in sweats. Maybe the other students would be weird. Scratch that, they would definitely be weird. What had she been thinking? She glanced in the window, checking her hair in the reflection. She caught the eye of a boy sitting inside. He waved. Shit. No turning back now.

Tucking her curly brown hair behind her ears, she stepped in. The boy who'd been eyeing her had a small smile tugging at the corner of his lips. The others sat in a circle of desks, turning simultaneously to take her in. Mar swallowed the nerves balled up in her throat.

"Um, hey, this is bird club, right?" She looked desperately over at the teacher, who sat behind a desk near the whiteboard and didn't bother to raise her eyes from the book in her lap.

"Bird*watching* club," said a girl with long silver hair and dark eye makeup. "Five bird nerds and Ms. Plummer, who couldn't tell a heron from a crane if it stole the romance novel out from her hands."

"Hilarious, Lena," Ms. Plummer said, still not raising her eyes from the page. She gestured vaguely at the middle of the room, presumably for Mar to take a seat.

The boy who'd been staring pulled a desk over to his side, swiveled it around to join the circle.

"You new here?"

He pushed his glasses up the bridge of his nose and cocked an eyebrow.

Mar felt a response come to her lips and then, to her horror, nothing came out.

The boy's legs were spread wide like the classroom was his. He was annoyingly hot.

"I'm Xavier," he tried again. He twisted a finger through the ends of his Afro absentmindedly.

"Mar," she finally managed.

She pulled her backpack into her lap and then, realizing she was gripping it so tightly the blood vanished from her fingertips, she placed it slowly on the floor.

"I just moved here," Mar said. "From San Jose. My dad is Gabriel Amado. He teaches——"

"No way! You're Mr. Amado's daughter?" Lena said excitedly. "I'm in his social studies class. He's the chillest teacher here. Except for Ms. Plummer, of course," she added loudly.

Ms. Plummer snorted and kept her eyes on her book.

Lena gave her a rundown of the club: they met once a week after school and tallied any new bird sightings. Sometimes they shared articles about local migration patterns or climate threats. On weekends, they went for hikes in Tilden Park to birdwatch. And they kept a running log of all the birds they'd spotted, as well as the elusive ones they still hadn't managed to lay eyes on.

Mar stayed quiet for most of the hour, observing. Lena and Xavier argued about the merits of the scrub jay (blue wings, white belly, wicked caw) versus the Steller's jay (blue wings, black belly, sick mohawk). Lena let out a loud cry, imitating the sound of a crow she'd come across on her way to school. The others burst out laughing, and Mar's stomach clenched with jealousy at their obvious ease with one another. And then, to Mar's surprise and intense secondhand embarrassment, the others broke out into their own chorus of caws, hoots, and trills, imitating other birds. Xavier caught Mar's eye and hooted. They were definitely weird, but maybe they were just the kind of weird she needed.

At the end of the hour, as everyone got up to leave, Mar heard a loud crack. She cast her eyes down to the floor and spotted a journal, a messy scrawl of notes and sketches peeking out from between its folds. Without thinking, she reached down and brought the book into her lap. Turning the pages slowly, she gaped at the intricate detail of an eagle's crooked toes curled around a branch, the long beak of a sandpiper dipping into the receding tide.

"Ahem."

Mar glanced up to see Xavier standing above her, his hand held out.

"Oh, sorry," she stammered, handing the book over. She immediately regretted her apology, hearing her mother's voice in her head telling her never to apologize unless she'd actually done something wrong, especially to a boy. He was the one who'd dropped the book, after all.

"Like what you see?" Xavier said, grinning.

Mar remembered herself and raised an eyebrow.

"It's all right, I guess," she said, tossing her backpack over her shoulder.

Xavier's smile wavered as she turned and walked out of the room. She knew how to deal with cocky boys. She might need new friends, badly. But this guy . . . The last thing she needed was the kind of distraction he would be.

Mar had promised herself before the year started, if she was going to change schools and upend her whole life, it had to be for one reason: she was going to get straight As, write a killer application, and get into her dream college. She had her eyes on the climate justice program at Brown University. She just had to stay focused. Less boy drama, more AP Bio.

"So, *Mar*—is that short for something?"

Xavier jogged up behind her.

"Kind of," she said, scanning the numbers on the long hall of lockers. "My dad's mom was Maria del Sol. But I'm just Mar."

"That's cool," Xavier said, adjusting his stride to fall into step beside her. "And you live around here?"

"Like a mile away, maybe?" Mar said distractedly. What was

her locker number again? Thirty-five, thirty-seven? "It's, like, a couple blocks from Cheese Board pizza."

Ah, thirty-nine. She remembered because that was her parents' age.

"No shit! That's pretty close to my house, actually," Xavier said, leaning against the locker next to hers.

"Cool." Mar jammed the key into her lock, jiggling it. Damn thing never opened when she needed it to.

"Yeah, I live up in the hills," Xavier said. "Maybe we can walk home together sometime. I'll show you the best boba on Shattuck."

Mar wriggled the key again, tugging down on the lock. Nothing. She groaned.

"May I?" Xavier said.

Mar stepped back. She watched Xavier's long fingers—smooth and delicate—play with the lock. Within seconds, she heard a click.

"There," he said, dropping it into her hand, their palms meeting a beat longer than was necessary. "So I guess I'll see you around?"

"I guess so," Mar said.

As Xavier walked off, his jeans hugged his legs in all the right places. Mar shook her head. *Don't go there.*

SEPTEMBER

The heat took its toll on the city, emanating up from the sidewalks, hanging in the air, drying the leaves and crackling the trees as they swayed in the wind. Tilden Park, usually an iridescent green bursting with eucalyptus groves, towering pines, and ferns filling the forest floor, was now a swath of patchy yellows and eerie grays.

Taylor ran on a secluded trail, bathed in sweat. Her steps left lines in the dusty, orange soil, pressing her footprints onto the earth's chapped lips.

She was thinking of how to break it to Abigail that she wanted to leave her.

"Honey, I'm not happy anymore," Taylor tried aloud. Too vague.

"Abby, if you hum when you chew your food one more time, I'm going to rip out your vocal cords with my bare hands." Too dramatic.

Climbing uphill, the tension building satisfyingly in her thighs, her feet leaping over gnarled roots and stray branches,

Taylor debated whether she should hold off until next summer, when Xavier would be headed to college, or just break it to Abigail now. Certainly, she could wait until after Abigail's birthday fundraiser shindig in a few weeks—she owed her wife that, at least. It annoyed Taylor to no end that Abigail had decided to turn her birthday, usually a quiet family affair, into a work event. But who was she to stop her wife from raising money for a good cause? She said nothing. Or rather, she said, "Sure, that sounds fine, Abby." Turned back to her coffee. Cracked open the paper. Less pressure on her to plan something special, she supposed.

Taylor turned off the main trail and darted into one of the narrow paths, threading deeper into the woods. Here, the eucalyptus provided shade from the sun's oppressive beams. The trees' peeling bark revealed stripes of dark coffee, chestnut, and pale green, a plant determined to continually shed its old self to become something new.

"We shouldn't have to live like this, Abby. Only moderately happy. We only have one life." Too cliché.

As the trail narrowed, crisscrossed brambles and dead branches crinkled under her feet. Taylor wiped cobwebs from the path to jog farther in.

The problem was, Taylor couldn't really explain, even to herself, why their life made her only moderately happy. Or rather, quietly, intensely, furiously unhappy. She didn't think Abigail would understand if she tried to spell it out, all the ways that Taylor had chipped away pieces of herself to get to where they were. She knew how it looked from the outside: she had everything she could possibly want—a steady partner, a healthy child, a beautiful home in the Berkeley Hills. And yet, somehow, she couldn't help but feel that she'd spent much of her adult life building toward a picturesque shell of an existence, which left her hollowed out.

Taylor stopped to catch her breath, feeling the anxiety

bubbling up as she thought about Xavier's parent-teacher meeting that night. It was one of those painfully performative Berkeley High events, where she and Abigail would play the proud parents, only to ride home in the car afterward in a numb silence. These gatherings, which were supposed to be about the children, always ended up being about the adults: each one assessing the other, deciding whose life was falling apart enough to provide fresh gossip fodder, whose child was destined for Ivy League greatness and whose doomed to an unknown college or—God forbid—no college at all. Taylor loathed the evenings most of all for the inevitable moment when, meeting a new parent, they might ask what she did for a living. And in a split second, she had to decide, depending on her mood and just how sharply dressed the person across from her was, whether to go with *I'm a full-time mom* or *I'm taking some time off after selling my start-up*. Both were true, technically, if "some time off" could mean fifteen years.

If Taylor said she was a stay-at-home mom, she'd have to endure the women—it was always women, the ones in crisp, tailored suits—who smiled too widely: "How wonderful—truly the hardest work!" Their enthusiasm did a poor job of masking their disdain. If Taylor said she was on a break post-acquisition, she got the temporary satisfaction of watching their lips part, their eyes pop wide as they nodded in barely suppressed envy. But then she had to live with, seconds later, the bitter taste that climbed up her throat, her own acid disgust at having admitted publicly—and worst of all, to herself—that somehow it wasn't enough for her to just be Xavier's mom. That she wanted more.

Taylor stopped running, leaning against a live oak tree to catch her breath. Her feet were tangled in a foot-high layer of knotted shrubs coating the forest floor. As she looked around, it dawned on her that she couldn't really tell where she'd come in from. Her pulse quickened as she twisted from side to side, trying to see which direction to head back out. She laughed bitterly at the irony.

It had been on a similar dirt path, almost two decades ago, in the narrow forest along the edge of Golden Gate Park, that she had come up with the idea for her start-up: a simple map, except instead of displaying streets, it marked trails for runners and hikers. The Bay was full of potential users, avid trekkers relying on word of mouth or stumblings-upon to travel the hundreds of pathways snaking through San Francisco, Oakland, Berkeley, and Marin. As a woman—a Black woman, specifically—Taylor could never quite let loose while jogging along lesser-known trails, unsure of where she was going, what kind of neighborhood she might pop out in as the sun set and the unfamiliar surroundings grew harder to decipher. Hence, a map. Predictable, point A to point B. Safe.

She built it up in a few years, and then, to her unending surprise, it was bought out for a mind-boggling amount of money—so much so that Abigail was able to quit her soul-sucking job in corporate law to move into nonprofit work, and Taylor was able to stop working altogether to raise their son. It felt, at the time, like they'd achieved everything they could have hoped for: more meaningful endeavors for them both. More time beyond the grind. More freedom. And yet.

Somehow Taylor had ended up feeling like the maps she'd so diligently designed: predictable, safe. Complacent.

The leaves rustled lightly around her, a peaceful sound grown menacing in her disorientation. For God's sake, she admonished herself. You know this place by heart. She turned in circles, dry twigs and branches clawing at her ankles, drawing blood. A bead of sweat ran down her back and, mistaking it for an insect, Taylor slapped at herself. How had she gotten lost somewhere so familiar?

It dawned on her then, a gradual descent into shifting sands, that all of the things she'd managed to achieve—her degrees, her company—the things she'd acquired—a house in the hills, antique tables, and outrageously priced armchairs—and the things she'd nurtured—her marriage, her son—somehow hadn't added up to what she'd imagined they would: a sense of ease, perhaps. Of happiness, certainly. Of fulfillment. It felt unfair really, like she'd been tricked. Wasn't this what one was supposed to strive for in life? What else was there?

She thought of the afternoons she'd spent with little Xavier after she stopped working. She'd watch their son play in the sandbox at the playground for hours, marveling at how he shared his shovel and pail, welling with pride at the engineering savvy already visible in his elaborate sandcastles. At first, Taylor felt an almost embarrassing luxury in being able to spend all day with her child. But then, over time, there crept up an altogether different sensation: she grew bored.

She tried to get back into her field—came up with new ideas, pitched them to her contacts. The executives dismissed her best one out of hand: another map, this time to locate the nearest diaper-changing stations for parents on the go. The concept was "too niche," they said, the market of potential users "too narrow." What they meant was that she was too much a mother now, had lost her edge—shrunken, somehow, by all that nursing and burping and ass-wiping (which, frankly, was far less than the coddling and fake-smiling and ass-kissing she'd had to do in tech, but no matter). She turned back to parenting with a fierce determination—making sure Xavier got into the best schools, enrolled in the right extracurriculars, attended the most prestigious summer camps. What could another app hold up to the value of raising a whole human being anyhow?

Before she knew it, fifteen years had passed and she had poured so much of her energy into crafting Xavier's life that she'd left little for her own. Somehow, among all the milestones hit and the boxes checked, she'd lost herself.

Taylor hunched over, wheezing, trying to fill her lungs with more oxygen. She couldn't tell if her chest was tight from the throat-clinging heat or from the overwhelming urge she felt to leave it all behind—the expectations of her as a mother; the tiresome dance of dodging Abigail's worried gaze around the house; the incessant thought that there was another life for her, somewhere out there, if only she was brave enough to release this one.

The thought circled her brain, relentless and cloying, like a hair caught in a drain: *You could leave . . . or you could stay and keep living this unhappy life. Up to you.*

Suddenly, through the dripping bows of the eucalyptus branches, she saw it: a clearing. A narrow path and then the road. She burst forward, lifting her knees high in dramatic arches to evade the brambles, pulling twigs from her hair. A passing jogger frowned at her, startled by the disheveled-looking woman emerging from the forest's depths. Taylor smiled, embarrassed. She jogged slowly at first, and then sprinted all-out toward home.

As she passed the creek running along the valley floor, she read the sign hanging on the fence: NO DOGS IN WATER. PROTECTED HABITAT FOR CALIFORNIA TROUT. Except there was no water left to speak of. No trout. It had stopped raining months ago. Taylor couldn't remember the last time she'd seen even a trickle there. She wondered where all the fish had gone. If they swam upstream to fuller rivers and lakes. Or if they got caught suddenly one morning, the creek bed they called home just a pathetic trail of mud. She imagined the fish flopping on their backs, eyes wide in panic, choking on air.

———

A few blocks past the teens playing pickup at the courts in San Pablo Park, beyond the bright yellow house with magenta window trim on Channing Way that made one wonder if the owners hadn't regretted the color as soon as the paint dried, inside the tall gates that bordered Berkeley High's campus, Xavier stood at the cafeteria door, peering in. He was trying to decipher on his moms' faces whether Mr. Amin had told them just how distracted he'd been in algebra class lately.

It was parent-teacher conference night, and part of Xavier didn't care. He'd be off to college soon anyway. But another part of him had grown accustomed to his mothers' praise, couldn't go without it now.

The problem was, in algebra, in birdwatching club—basically anywhere he and Mar existed in remotely the same vicinity— Xavier couldn't think straight. As soon as she walked into a room, his whole body sensed it. Without even having to look up, a current of electricity ran through him, all his skin cells alight, and it took every ounce of self-control for him to appear unflustered, to remain chill.

Earlier that day, in Mr. Amin's class, Xavier had been diligently solving for x, carrying the digits from one side of the equation to the other, when he heard the scrape of a chair behind him, the unmistakable squeak of Mar's sneakers against the linoleum floor. He saw the shape of her in the corner of his eye as she passed his seat. He kept still, only lifting his head once she had walked by. He trained his eyes on the back of her neck, on the spot where her thick, dark hair, tied up in a bun, left a stray curl loose. As Mar spat her gum out into the trash can, Xavier felt an overwhelming urge to run over and pick it up out of the bin. He would stick it in his mouth, bite down, squeeze out the juices of her saliva, swallowing her. But he wasn't a total freak. He didn't move, glancing up only once Mar was a few feet ahead of him, nodding at her coolly, a slight smile at his lips that was meant to say, *hey, what's up*—casual, no big deal. She smiled back. When he looked down at his page, he was lost. He had no clue where he'd left off, none of the numbers made sense, his writing was a blur. His head overflowed with her.

"Hey, X."

Xavier jumped. Mar was standing behind him, a stack of books in her arms, as usual.

"Oh, hey, Mar."

He said it with the rolled *r*, like in Spanish, and immediately regretted it. He sounded like an idiot.

He'd been trying to come up with a nickname for her—the way she'd spontaneously started calling him X, which made him feel special, like he meant something to her. But there were only so many nicknames for a one-syllable name. He'd tried Mari. Margarita. Even Marshmallow. It was all deeply humiliating.

Mar peered beyond him into the room where their parents were gathering data from their teachers, searching for assurances that they'd done a good job, that their kids were all right. Xavier felt her body leaning toward his, could smell the coconut in her hair. He didn't move. Playing it cool around Mar was a practice in stillness. Like when he was birdwatching and heard the telltale tap of a Nuttall's woodpecker against a tree. Once he caught a flash of the bird's bright red crown and black wings, he stood stock-still, turning slowly, making as little sound as possible, waiting. As badly as he wanted to get closer, he didn't dare startle it away.

"Your parents in there?" Xavier asked, nudging his glasses up the bridge of his nose, a nervous tic.

"Yeah," Mar said, leaning against the wall of lockers.

Xavier could see tiny beads of sweat gathering on her upper lip. It was stifling in the hallway. The heat looked good on her. He forced his eyes back up to meet hers.

"Honestly, it's been so long since my parents have been in the same room," Mar said. "I'm checking to make sure they're not fighting or some shit."

"That bad?" he said. Her eyes flicked to him, and he felt a rush of heat to his cheeks. He hoped she didn't notice.

"Sometimes, yeah."

Xavier still couldn't quite read Mar. He counted the days until he saw her in birdwatching club: long weekends, and then a brief respite on Mondays in Mr. Amin's class, followed by the rest of the week dragging on with only the occasional glance or smile in the hallway, and finally Thursday evenings, birdwatching club. He spent far too many hours strategizing what he'd wear that day. Something chill, laid-back—an old T-shirt with a nineties band on it, or a flannel rolled up at the sleeves. It had to look effortless, like he wasn't trying too hard. Which of course he was. Always. He timed himself to arrive at the meeting room late, to make sure she got there first, so he could pull up a desk beside her. There were times when he thought that she might be into him, too. She laughed at his bad jokes, and occasionally touched him when she didn't need to—pulling his sketchbook into her lap to flip through his latest illustrations, asking him for his sweater that one time when it was chilly. But other times, if he got too flirtatious, she pulled away, deflecting his come-ons with a sarcastic comment or, worse, her pensive silences. Maybe she was playing hard to get. But there was also the possibility— and a pit of anxiety bloomed in his stomach at the thought—that she just wasn't into him. Which would really blow.

Mar locked eyes with Xavier. "Do you ever feel like you're a magnet, and your parents are . . . metal, maybe, and each of them is stuck to you, but also pulling at you, like they want so much of you—or for you—that you're being torn apart?"

Xavier frowned. The way Mar spoke sometimes, he stumbled

through her words, mesmerized and a bit confused, the full meaning floating just beyond his reach. He struggled to come up with an answer, wanting to make sure she felt understood, but also not quite knowing what to say.

"Never mind. Maybe it's a divorced-parents thing." She looked past him again.

"No, I get it," Xavier said quickly.

And on second thought, he did. His moms weren't split up, but sometimes, when they were watching a movie, Mama Taylor and Mom Abby sat on either side of him and neither of them said a word to the other. They both glanced at him occasionally, as though to make sure he was enjoying himself. And he sat still, pretending not to notice. When they fought—they never yelled, rarely even raised their voices—he played the ball boy at a tennis match, watching them serve up volleys, each one sharper than the last, until one of them, usually Mama, spiked the ball, finishing Mom off. Then Mom would search the room for Xavier, seeking his alliance. And he'd stand there, balls scattered across the court, hedging his words, trying not to give either of them a reason to feel alone.

Xavier kicked himself for always thinking too much and not saying enough.

As he stared at Mar, he thought that if he could want someone, and also want to be them, to devour every inch of their body, touching and smelling and licking them until all of his senses were filled with them, then that's what he felt for her. Like he could consume her whole and still not get enough.

"Shit, they're talking to the college counselor," Mar said.

"Oh. That's whatever." Xavier swiped the air casually. Confident, chill.

"So, what—you're not worried about getting into college?"

He bit the inside of his cheek, drawing blood. Obviously, he was worried. He didn't know why he was pretending not to be. Xavier spent so much of his life performing what he thought people wanted of him that sometimes, he didn't even know what he wanted himself. Mom Abby wanted him to have good grades, so he did. Mama Taylor wanted him to be happy, so he acted as though he was. The guys at school wanted him to laugh at their jokes, even when they made digs about his Blackness, or his Jewishness, or both. Xavier smiled and shrugged it off. Nobody liked a killjoy.

But Mar felt like the opposite of all that. She was studious as hell and had no patience for other people's bullshit. When Derek asked her in gym class if she ran so fast because she was used to dodging bullets in her old neighborhood, Mar stopped, looked at him, and said: "You think gun violence is funny? That's pretty fucked up." The other students froze. Someone oohed. Derek chuckled and said, "Whatever," under his breath. But no one tried anything with her after that.

"No, for sure, I'm worried," Xavier said. "I just . . . already made up my mind about where I want to go."

Mar nodded. "Me too, actually. Brown has this climate justice program. I'd kill to get in."

Xavier laughed. "No way! My top choice is RISD."

Mar frowned.

"The art school? RISD and Brown have adjoining campuses," Xavier said. "They didn't talk about that on your tour?"

"Oh." The crease between her brows deepened. "I didn't do a tour, actually. I've never been."

"Right, yeah." Why did he always say the wrong thing? He mumbled something about college visits being a bore anyway, how his moms made him do eight campuses in two days and they all blurred together by the end. Mar said nothing.

"That'd be cool, though, right? If we both got in," Xavier said. "We could birdwatch together."

But Mar was staring past him again.

Xavier turned around. There was Mar's dad, Mr. Amado, walking toward them. A woman was with him, the spitting image of Mar, only older. And ten steps behind them were his moms.

———

At the end of the school day, his twelfth-grade social studies class mercifully behind him, Gabriel Amado ducked into the teachers' lounge and tried to summon the energy for the evening ahead. He changed into a fresh button-down, only to look in the mirror and take it off again, trying on a polo instead. He was going to see Camila for the first time in months. He wanted to look good, like someone who had his life together. Like he was doing just fine without her.

When Camila walked into the cafeteria, Gabriel was glad that he'd settled on the dark polo that slimmed his waistline. She was as stunning as ever. It wasn't so much that her face was so obviously beautiful (it was). It was her presence, the confident way she took up space in a room, which made it impossible for his eyes to land anywhere else.

"Hey, gordo," Camila said. She gave Gabriel a casual peck on the cheek. His armpits began to sweat again. He didn't know if it was from the nerves or the heat.

Of course, Camila had shown up in the same bold red lip and formfitting jeans she wore every day. Camila didn't change to fit a situation—the situation had better fit itself to her.

At moments like these, Gabriel questioned why exactly they'd split up. There was his cheating, of course, but hadn't there also been a bunch of other things that led up to that? The way that, over the years, he'd grown to feel like Camila didn't really need him. How she sometimes looked at him like he was a disappointment. He hadn't just up and left. He'd been pushed out long before. Hadn't he?

They sat in small plastic chairs across from Ms. Carpenter, who beamed, telling them that Mar's report on fossil fuels was one of the best she'd seen in her two decades as an educator. In fact, it left her feeling so awful that she was considering canoeing to Portland over Thanksgiving rather than risk the carbon footprint of taking a plane. She chuckled and Gabriel laughed along. Camila smiled in her usual, assured way, like she knew of her daughter's brilliance, didn't need it confirmed. After they finished their rounds—Mar was "excellent," "whip-smart," "eloquent" (Camila raised an eyebrow at that one)—they made their way to the exit. And before Gabriel knew it, they were arguing, again. The college counselor had assured them that Mar had the grades to get into Brown. But she wasn't sure if she would qualify for a full ride, given Gabriel's and Camila's modest but not entirely insignificant incomes as public schoolteachers. Gabriel thought that if Mar got in, she should absolutely go, come hell or high water, even if it meant taking out more loans. He remembered being her age and how badly he wanted to get out of Fresno. He wanted the whole world to open up to their girl. But Camila argued that Ivy Leagues weren't the only institutions offering a great education, that they should prioritize Mar not graduating saddled by a mountain of student debt, like the ones they were still climbing out from under. Camila was just switching from English to Spanish—all the better to chew him out in public with—when they saw Mar.

She was standing in the hall next to a boy that Gabriel had seen before around school. He was tall and lanky, clearly still coming into his body in the way teenage boys were, his face all wide-framed glasses, picked-out Afro, and a vague attempt at facial hair. And he was looking at Mar like she was the sun and he was lucky to get to bask in her light. Camila shot Gabriel a look of *this isn't over*, and they pasted on smiles.

"How's mi muñeca?" Gabriel said, wrapping an arm around Mar. He gave the boy an assertive nod.

Mar was wearing her BRUJA CHICANA T-shirt, and Gabriel felt a twinge of jealousy. Camila was fierce about passing on her Mexican heritage, and Gabriel knew it wasn't a competition, but also, after a divorce, it was hard not to get into the mindset that their kid was a finite resource and the more of himself he could squeeze in, the better. He wanted Mar to feel just as connected to Ecuador, to his side of the family. Maybe he'd take her to Quito over spring break, introduce her to the Andean hillsides her abuelos grew up in. Those mountains were like nowhere she'd ever seen, dotted with brightly colored houses, the clouds resting below the tallest peaks in the early morning, a bed for the gods.

"Papi, Mami, this is my friend X," Mar said, gesturing to her bespectacled admirer.

"X, eh?" Gabriel said, turning toward the boy. "Do you have telepathic powers, Professor?"

Camila rolled her eyes at Gabriel's X-Men joke, and Mar cringed: "Papi."

Xavier gratifyingly broke into a smile and said, "You know mutants can't reveal their powers like that."

Gabriel chuckled and bowed his head as though conceding the point.

"And who is this?" said a cheery voice from behind him.

Gabriel turned to see two middle-aged women, both in the same uniform of oversize button-down shirts and linen pants. The women hugged Xavier, who squirmed.

"Moms, this is Mar, my . . . friend from birdwatching club. And these are her parents, Mr. Amado and . . ." The boy's eyes popped wide as he realized he didn't know Camila's name.

"Camila," she said, chuckling, offering a hand to shake.

"Nice to meet you," one of the women said, introducing herself as Taylor, and her wife as Abigail. "Mar, we've heard so much about you at home."

Xavier's face twisted into a mask of intense mortification. Gabriel worried the boy might pass out.

"And what is it that you do?" Abigail said, smiling.

"I'm a teacher here, actually," Gabriel said. "I recently got a place nearby, and lucky for me, Mar agreed to move from her mom's in San Jose to spend her senior year living with me, her smelly old pops!"

Camila's lips tightened almost imperceptibly.

Gabriel reached up and pinched Mar's cheek. She swatted his hand away and stuck out her tongue.

"And you?" Gabriel asked.

"I work in affordable housing," Abigail said, with a smile Gabriel couldn't help but read as self-satisfied. He resisted turning to see if Camila had registered it.

"I'm . . ." Taylor paused for a split second. "A full-time mom."

"Wonderful," Gabriel said.

"You'll let us know if we can be of any help," Abigail said, placing a hand on Gabriel's forearm. "We've lived in Berkeley for ages, so we know the whole school system inside out."

"Oh, thank you, that's all right," Camila cut in. "I'm a teacher, too, so we've got a good handle on it."

Gabriel wondered if the other women could hear the tension in Camila's voice or if he'd only come to recognize it from years of deciphering her every micro-movement.

"You know, actually, we're having a little get-together in a few weeks," Abigail said. "It's a fundraiser for a housing project I'm working on. It also happens to be my birthday, but that's neither here nor there. You should come! There will be a ton of other Berkeley parents; you can meet the whole crew."

"Oh, thank you, we'd love to," Gabriel said, just as Camila said: "We're good—thank you, though."

Taylor, clearly holding back a laugh, tugged Abigail toward the door. "We should head out. If you do end up making it, it will be great to see you again."

Abigail winked at Gabriel, adding in a faux-hushed tone: "I'll have Xavier give Mar the deets."

Once they were out of earshot, Gabriel turned to Camila: "Why can't you just be nice? These are parents at the school I work at. Parents of Mar's friend, por Dios!"

"You and I both know who these people are, Gabriel," Camila said, using his full name like she only did when she was upset. "What does that woman think, she owns this school? *Please, come to my humble cocktail party, I shall introduce you to the people who matter.*"

"It wasn't like that and you know it," Gabriel said. "Sabes, not everything is a slight."

"No, of course not. And certainly not if it's coming from one of your school's parents." Camila wrapped a hand through the crook of Mar's arm and spun their daughter toward the exit. "Adiós, Gabriel."

Gabriel pursed his lips. As they walked off—Mar tossing an apologetic smile over her shoulder (she was sleeping at her mom's tonight)—Gabriel wondered if there really was something he'd missed, or if this was, once again, Camila finding him insufficient, too naive for this world. Well, it didn't matter. He had his new apartment, with peeling paint and a clanky ceiling fan, but nothing he couldn't fix when he got the time. He was building a new life. She'd see.

PART II

air

OCTOBER

The sky hung low over the Bay, a thin haze descending slowly. Some twenty-odd miles north, inland from the coast, the flames of a fire were budding, crackling through the woods, no witnesses but the birds and the deer. Overnight, the fumes had curled upward and traveled south, growing wispier with each mile as they crept toward Berkeley. The city's inhabitants woke to a blurriness outside, a vague scent of char, the sky dotted with barely visible ash. If they breathed it in for too long, it started to feel like so many fingers closing around their throats. Most people were unfazed, used to such occurrences in the midst of fire season. It had been hot for weeks, after all. Dry for months. It made sense. Some checked the air quality index, others moved their evening plans indoors, fewer still turned air purifiers on. Many simply moved on with their days.

Taylor sat at the kitchen island, running through her to-do list: She'd planned dinner and bought the groceries. She'd put away Xavier's laundry, which he'd tossed in a heap on his bedroom floor. She'd even begun to wipe down the windowsills, which had collected an unusual thin layer of soot overnight, before she remembered the house cleaner was coming the next day. She wasn't sure what else to do. Xavier was at school and Abigail at work, busy closing a deal on a new affordable housing complex. Taylor was, once again, alone at home, faced with herself.

She looked at the frames hanging on the living room wall, all different sizes and colors, strategically placed to appear eclectic, not too polished. There was an old photo of the three of them at Baker Beach—Xavier grinning, a smile full of baby teeth; Abigail looking at Taylor, beaming; and Taylor smiling vaguely, staring off toward the coast. Taylor couldn't remember the last time she'd paid such close attention to the photo. Over time, it had blended into the background of their home, a happy moment captured and set behind glass, and then forgotten, not tended to.

Taylor sighed and reluctantly made her way to her laptop. She opened it to a page she'd been staring at off and on for weeks, not daring to type anything further. It was an email she'd drafted to some of the people she knew from her start-up days, pitching them a new idea: an eco-friendly children's clothing line. Each item would be designed to allow the child to grow into it as they aged—strategically placed zippers, stretchy waistbands, Velcro expanders to accommodate small limbs growing long. The idea was to reduce waste for the environment and parents' budgets. Done right, it could change the children's clothing industry— forget that, upend fast fashion altogether. But as Taylor went to click SEND, she hovered over the names of the recipients: the same executives—the same men—who'd dismissed her idea of a map of diaper-changing stations all those years ago. She felt the hot shame of failure sizzling in her chest. She slammed the laptop shut.

Outside, the sky was tinted gray, a fog-like haze curling through the trees surrounding their house, closing in. She couldn't sit here any longer.

She got in the car and drove off. As she passed Tilden Park, a sign whizzed by:

PARK CLOSED DUE TO HIGH FIRE RISK.

NO PEDESTRIANS ON TRAILS.

EMERGENCY VEHICLES ONLY.

Before she knew it, she was pulling up outside a familiar building. She hesitated before placing a call.

Xavier came jogging out from Berkeley High, frowning in confusion.

"Hey, Mama," he said, leaning into her car window. "Everything all right?"

"All good," Taylor said, smiling, papering over the panic lodged in her chest. "I just thought . . . Want to play hooky for the day? Just you and me."

Xavier's frown deepened. "Um, I don't know if you've met my mother. Her name is Taylor Hayes. She's pretty serious about my attending school."

"Hardy-har. I would have thought you'd jump at the chance to get out of class. What's one day away?"

Xavier glanced back at the building, seeming to hesitate. Then he opened the car door. "You better drive off before my mama changes her mind."

They sped across the bridge, miraculously free of traffic in the middle of a weekday. Xavier took his sneakers off and placed his feet on the dashboard, emboldened by Taylor's abandon. Stevie Wonder played on the radio, and they sang along, humming the lyrics they couldn't recall and belting the ones they knew by heart.

Without thinking, Taylor drove straight to Baker Beach, where her father used to take her as a child, and where she and Abigail later took Xavier. When the weather was warm enough, they rolled up their pants, let the Pacific rush over their toes, cleansing them of their worries.

Taylor took her shoes off, left them in the car. She stepped onto the sand and felt it smoothing out the soles of her feet as they walked. Cliffs hung over the beach, dotted with tall white and yellow houses. As a girl, she used to fantasize about living in one of those, decks spilling out over a beautiful void. Her father wondered aloud at what on earth the owners could possibly do for a living. "They mustn't have a care in the world," he said, watching a man lean up against the glass railing, his face aglow with the sun's rays ducking into the ocean.

Now Taylor knew, as someone with her own house, its own deck with a breathtaking view, just how wrong her father was.

"In your wildest dreams," Taylor said, turning to Xavier, "what would you want to be when you grow up?"

Xavier nudged his glasses up the bridge of his nose. "I want to work in tech, I think," he said. "Maybe build a birding app. One where you could just upload a photo of any bird you saw in the wild, or even just a recording of its call, and it would tell you what kind of bird it was, its migration patterns, how rare the sighting. Every bird in the world in the palm of your hand."

"Very cool," Taylor said. "You know, I built an app myself, once upon a time."

"I know," Xavier said, smiling mischievously. "So tell me why it is I still need to show you how to drag your photos from your phone onto the cloud."

"Why, you little . . ." Taylor poked a finger into Xavier's side.

He laughed and sprinted up the beach. Taylor ran after him, her pant legs soaking in the rising tide.

As she jogged, she felt her chest tighten. Her breath came in shorter bursts. She stopped and bent over, heaving in a coughing fit. The smoke was getting to her, irritating her asthma.

Xavier came running back.

She brushed away his concern: "It's okay, baby. Tell me something to distract me from this heinous air." They walked back toward the car.

After a pause, Xavier said: "Well, there is this girl at school I'm kind of into."

Taylor knew exactly who he was talking about.

On parent-teacher conference night, her son had looked at that girl, Mar, as though if she'd asked, he would have lain down on a bed of hot coals, let her walk over his every limb, searing the longing into his body, just to spare her feet any discomfort. Taylor had never seen her boy gaze at someone like that. He'd felt suddenly older to her then. Somehow further away. She was thrilled for him, and sad all at once, the brutal passage of time settling itself like a weight on her chest.

"I guess I don't know how to tell if we're just friends or if she likes me like that, you know?" he said.

Taylor thought of when she'd first met Abigail. Taylor's sorority was hosting a coat drive after winter break at Smith. She was tasked with accepting donations at the booth when a girl with dark eyes and long brown hair kept showing up, over and over, with more coats. First, she brought by a long tweed jacket. Then she dropped off a couple puffy numbers with fuzzy trim around the hoods. Finally, when she left a fur coat, Taylor burst out laughing. "I'm sorry, where the hell are you getting all of these?" The girl looked at her, startled. She broke into a smile. "Well, I saw you sitting here, collecting these coats, and I realized I'm probably not going to be needing my winter stuff after I graduate, since I'm moving to California. And then I thought of all the other East Coasters who got jobs out west. So I started harassing my friends to give me their coats, too. And here we are." Taylor chuckled. "I'm from San Francisco," she said. "You know it's still pretty damn cold there in the winter, right?" The girl froze, her eyes wide. "Well, don't tell anyone else here that." Taylor chuckled. She hesitated, then told the girl she'd be around until late, "in case you find any more windbreakers to siphon off unknowing seniors." The girl left. When she came back, she was carrying another coat, and two hot chocolates.

"Invite Mar to do something with you. Something that fills you up," Taylor said. "There's nothing sexier than watching someone do what they love."

Xavier shivered dramatically: "Mama. Please don't say 'sexy.'"

Taylor laughed.

On the drive home, they sat in an easy silence. Taylor wondered how it could be that she and Abigail had gone from constantly, casually touching each other—a hand resting on the back of the other's neck, a foot tucked in between the other's calves—to Taylor feeling tense whenever Abigail came into a room, anticipating her own annoyance before her wife even opened her mouth. Taylor knew she was misplacing her frustrations on Abigail. It wasn't Abigail's fault, after all, that Taylor's life hadn't turned out to be . . . well, she wasn't quite sure what. But she also didn't know how to untangle Abigail from it all. Not when her wife seemed so satisfied.

Taylor felt as though she had poured every grain of sand from her body into the glass jar of their shared life—building their financial security, raising their child, keeping their home—shoveling in more and more of herself, year after year, not realizing that she was burying herself in the process.

"When we get home, I'll make us pancakes," Taylor said. "Breakfast for dinner, like old times."

Xavier shifted in his seat. "Actually, I was wondering if you could drop me back at school? I don't want to miss birdwatching club."

"Oh, of course," Taylor said, a fissure cracking wider in her chest. "Good for you."

Alone again, Taylor drove back into the hills, impatiently wiping at the tears that stained her cheeks. If she had driven off that morning, dragged Xavier out of school, raced to the water's edge, to quell a violent urge to escape the mundane trappings of her house, now, crying to "I Just Called to Say I Love You," alone in her car, all Taylor wanted to do was be back at home.

When she stepped into the kitchen, she found Abigail standing at the island, staring out into the haze. Taylor looked at her wife, the way Abigail's hand moved up to brush her bangs away from her crease-lined forehead. All of her intentions shriveled up in her throat. The words she had practiced—*I want to leave you*—gathered in her mouth and dropped back down her esophagus, sliding into the pit of her stomach.

Taylor walked over and wrapped her arms around Abigail from behind.

"Oh, hello," Abigail said, startled—Taylor didn't know if by her sudden presence or by her touch.

Taylor spun her wife around and kissed her. Abigail's lips were soft and pliable. Taylor pulled her in more urgently, grabbing her by the juicy flesh of her hips, searching for something in her grasp.

Abigail pulled back and cocked an eyebrow at Taylor in mock surprise.

Taylor stiffened. She turned away, not wanting to stare down the scarcity of her affection.

"Did you hear on the radio about the fire?" Taylor said, opening the freezer door, feeling the relief of the cool air on her face. "It's apparently getting close to Wildcat Canyon. The fire chief said that someday 'every acre of this state will burn.'"

Abigail frowned. "Well, that seems a bit melodramatic."

Taylor lingered, enjoying the sensation of the cold racing up her arms, all while anticipating Abigail's admonishment that she close the door and not waste power.

"The poor deer," Abigail mused. "They must be panicking, nowhere to run like that."

Taylor pursed her lips. "I don't know that the deer are the biggest concern here."

"Well, obviously not," Abigail said, reaching over and shutting the freezer door. "But I have the capacity for both. To care about the deer and the humans."

Taylor wordlessly opened the freezer again. She pulled out three ice cubes, dropped them into her empty glass, sharp clinks ringing out between them.

"Anyhow, I wouldn't worry too much," Abigail went on. "I looked it up and the last time there was a big fire in the East Bay was in the nineties. And that was in the Oakland Hills."

Oh, only the Oakland Hills. All right, then.

"Isn't that the point of climate change?" Taylor said, filling her cup. "That it's changing."

"I suppose." Abigail wiped down the edge of the sink where Taylor had splattered some water.

Taylor resisted the urge to grab the rag out of Abigail's hand, scrunch it into a ball, and shove it into her own mouth, muffling a scream.

She looked past Abigail out the window. Through the haze, she could only partially see the view they'd paid a dizzying $1.8 million for all those years ago.

"What are you thinking?" Abigail asked, hanging the rag on the oven door, smoothing it out.

Taylor thought that if she ever left, she would enjoy the ability to stay quiet for more than a minute at a time.

I'm thinking about leaving you.

"Nothing really," she said, turning toward the staircase. "I'm going to jump in the pool. Cool off."

"Okay." Abigail grabbed her tote off the counter. "I have to run to the bakery anyway."

Taylor went downstairs and stepped into the yard. She looked at the view and sighed. She could see the outline of all the tiny houses spread out below, the yellowing treetops hurtling toward the majestic expanse of the bay. Who could possibly be unhappy in a place like this? Her, apparently.

She hesitated only briefly before peeling off her pants and her shirt. Then her bra and her underwear. She didn't care if the neighbors saw her naked.

She took a deep breath and jumped, feeling the sun-drenched water surrounding her limbs, buoying them. She blew bubbles out in small bursts until she sank down to the pool's floor. Silence echoed in her ears, a balm. She closed her eyes. How long could she stay down here before someone noticed she was gone? How badly would it hurt if her lungs exploded? When would Abigail and Xavier realize—once dinner wasn't on at seven? When the table wasn't set and, ravenously hungry, they discovered she wasn't in the kitchen? She imagined Abigail frowning, calling out her name, stepping onto the deck, looking down and seeing her bloated body floating on the surface, bobbing in its unsightly, grayish tinge. Abigail's scream would ring out through the yards. But Taylor wouldn't hear a thing.

She felt her chest tighten and she kicked off the floor, gasping for air as she broke through the surface. She was slightly dizzy and a little exhilarated at having toyed with suffocation like that. Just another small way to feel alive.

———

Some three miles away, through the regal buildings and ancient eucalyptus groves of the University of California's Berkeley campus, past the frat houses lining Piedmont Avenue, across Claremont Avenue, with its brick mansions so imposing they couldn't possibly be family homes (they were), Willow sat on the corner of Domingo and Russell, her eyes closed, willing her slow-growing migraine away.

The heat was uncanny for October. All the hours sitting in the sun, inhaling ash-stained air, were starting to get to her. Aso lay lethargically at her feet, and Willow thought back to when fall in California wasn't so suffocating.

Growing up in Tahoe, she could count on the clear, crisp fall air ushering in a mellow winter. It was the best time of year, when her lakeside town finally got some respite from the rowdy summer people, a momentary pause before the skiers swarmed in. As the leaves turned, the interlopers evacuated her precious backwood trails, abandoned the hidden beach coves, cleared the waterfront of empty beer bottles and the incessant buzz of speedboats.

There was one upside to this time of year in Berkeley, she supposed: they didn't have to worry about rain leaking through the van's roof onto their mattress. Still, the haze gave the city a menacing glow, like she couldn't see a threat coming until it was too close.

A sudden pop followed by a tumble of tiny clangs startled Willow from her reverie.

"Oh, I'm sorry!" A middle-aged woman with short, dark hair

stood before her, partly hunched over, as though unsure whether to pick up the cup she had knocked over, spilling its coins and bills onto the sidewalk.

"Um, here you go," the woman said, frantically pulling a ten-dollar bill from her tote bag. The beige fabric read, GIVE A SHIT, DON'T EAT MEAT. The woman handed Willow the crumpled bill with an apologetic grimace.

"It's fine, don't worry about it," Willow mumbled, tucking the bill into her pocket.

As she scooped the fallen coins back into the cup's mouth, Willow blushed, feeling the stares of people standing in line at the French bakery across the street. By the time she scratched the last dimes and nickels out of a crack in the sidewalk, breaking the nail of her index finger in the process, the woman was halfway down the block.

She didn't know which was worse: the people who gave her pitying looks when she was panhandling, their brows all furrowed with concern, or the ones who walked right by, as though she didn't even exist.

Through the wide front window of Fournée Bakery, Willow could see row after row of baskets brimming with baguettes, neat wooden shelves holding up a dizzying array of breads, some dusted with flour, others dark to the point of appearing almost burnt. Willow's mouth filled with saliva, and she swallowed hard. She fingered the bill in her pocket.

Tying Aso to a tree—"Stay right here, good boy"—Willow marched across the street and stood in line. The people who'd been staring moments ago looked straight ahead.

When she got inside, the clang of the bell above the door startled her, as did the employee's cheery "Bonjour!" It was more crowded than she expected. Every square foot of the small black-and-white-tiled space was filled with someone reaching for a baguette, pointing at a loaf, or hovering over the glass pane of the pastry display. When her turn came, Willow stood in front of the neat rows of éclairs and croissants, struggling to make up her mind. She felt the pressure of the employee's strained smile, the not-so-subtle nudge of the next guest in line pressing up behind her. She took a deep breath and tried to focus. She was debating between the almond croissant ($4.25) or the lemon marmalade scone ($3.50) when, out of the corner of her eye, she spotted it: a perfectly glazed triangle of dark chocolate atop a moist sponge ($3.75).

"Two of those, please," she said, pressing her finger to the glass.

The bell clanged, and more people poured in. A surge of bodies surrounded her. Willow was hurtled back to a night many years ago, when she was squashed beneath someone else's body, when she couldn't breathe.

Willow pulled her hand back from the glass, placed it on her stomach. She was going to be sick.

"Anything else, miss?"

She grabbed the paper bag, placed the crumpled bill on the counter, and ran out the door. She didn't wait for her change. She sprinted across the street, ducked behind a tree, and vomited.

As she untied Aso, she didn't dare look back at the people in line, who were surely judging her, thinking that homeless woman was probably hungover or on drugs or something.

On her walk back to the van, she tried to remind herself that it was okay, it was fine if she didn't finish the day's collections. Sunny would understand. Still, she pinched herself for spending what little she'd gotten on two slices of cake, which were almost certainly melting at the bottom of the scrunched paper bag she was gripping. Maybe she wouldn't tell Sunny after all.

When she presented the gooey slices to him later that night, as they sat on the tiny sliver of sand along the water, Sunny asked where she'd managed to nab the unusual treats.

"The food bank," Willow lied.

She didn't have the energy to explain, to relay the story of the woman who kicked her cup and then paid her off for the transgression. And she felt even less up to the task of explaining how the line of customers, the sardine can of bodies in the bakery, too many limbs, too much hot breath, had sent her careening back to that night in Tahoe, when she'd shut her eyes, trying to force her imagination to float her away, off the cold tiled floor, anywhere but under the sweat-laced flesh pressing into her.

Willow took a fingerful of cake and shoved it into Sunny's half-open mouth, making him laugh. As his sputtering guffaw filled the air, she felt herself smile, too.

It was a sound she held on to, Sunny's laugh. On the days when the flashbacks of what she'd survived refused to stay in the recesses of her mind, when she thought she'd never again be able to hold down a steady job because of it, when the darkness felt like it might just pull her under once and for all (and what a respite that would be), Sunny's crinkly-eyed smile kept her anchored, kept her alive.

———

Gabriel stood at the front of his classroom, staring at the rows of twelfth graders, clearly too hot and too bored to pay much attention to anything he said. The hazy air poured through the school's archaic ventilation system, giving the space an even drearier quality than usual. He wondered briefly if this wasn't harmful for their health—all these young lungs, breathing in ashy particles, lining their insides with tar. But the problem of the building's infrastructure was above his pay grade. What he *could* control was what he had to offer to their sprouting, inquisitive minds.

And yet, even in that, he felt like a fraud. His students expected something from him—knowledge, maybe wisdom. Entertainment at least. But Gabriel had nothing.

"You think it's hot in *here*?" he tried, sweating unsightly rings down the back of his button-down shirt. He pulled up a slide with an image of César Chávez and Dolores Huerta. "Imagine what it was like to work the artichoke fields of the Central Valley in the nineteen sixties, in over one-hundred-degree heat!"

One of his students passed a note to a classmate, neither making much effort to conceal their inattention. Gabriel was too exhausted to call them out. He sighed and turned back to the whiteboard, writing out an assignment:

> *Imagine you were alive during the time of the United Farm*
> *Workers movement, doing backbreaking labor for little pay.*
> *Would you join the activists leading weeks-long fasts and strikes*
> *for better working conditions? Or would you stay on the job to*
> *not risk your pay and go hungry without wages, hoping to rise up*
> *in the ranks and earn more someday?*

Gabriel split the class in two, assigning each half of the room to argue one side of the question.

Lena, all silver hair and fiery opinions, immediately raised her hand.

"Why are we even arguing in favor of people working in shit conditions for shittier pay? Isn't it obvious they have to fight?" she said, staring at him with genuine confusion.

"Language, Lena," Gabriel said, unsure how else to respond. "Just complete the assignment, please."

The truth was, Gabriel didn't know what his own answer

would be. He didn't even sign the petition last year from the teachers' union calling for more mental health counselors in schools. To be fair, he'd been busy finalizing the divorce and applying for housing, and planning Mar's move to his place. But the truth was, he'd also just forgotten.

By the disappointed look on Lena's face, Gabriel guessed that she knew—that somehow they all knew—that Mr. Amado was full of shit, and he felt small and insignificant.

————

Winding up Euclid Avenue into the hills, Mar struggled to breathe through the smoke, ogling the houses—three-story Victorians with elegant, witchy pointed roofs, others more worn down, with faded slats, old peace-sign flags, and dusty cars in the driveway. Mar wondered what the ones with dizzyingly high fences were trying to hide. The gardens she could see were at once wild and contained, a plethora of succulents surrounding a lemon tree, the black snake of a semi-hidden irrigation system coiling beneath the leaves, a giveaway that this had all been carefully manicured. The higher they climbed, the greener the yards got, almost as though the hill dwellers hadn't gotten the memo that the state was in a drought. Maybe all the smoke had gone to their heads.

Xavier's hands swung at his sides, occasionally brushing hers. He'd invited her over to check out his feather collection. Mar didn't know why she'd said yes. She didn't want him getting the wrong idea. But also, if she was honest, she was lonely. Most days, she hung out with Lena, who was a trip and reminded her of her friends back home: boisterous and sarcastic, with zero filter. But Lena also had her own crew, and Mar didn't want to be too much of a hanger-on. And she liked Xavier. The more they hung out, the more his initial veneer of cool intimidation fell away. It turned out that he was just a huge nerd who got excited by being able to tell the difference between a Song Sparrow and a House Sparrow (the former was more dusky-colored with streaks of reddish brown along its wings, the latter painted with tiny strokes of black).

"What are you thinking?" Xavier asked.

She was thinking of the house with a skull hanging on its gate, a deer's or an elk's presumably. Mar imagined the owners stalking through the streets of the quiet neighborhood at night, slowly baiting the animal with hunks of lettuce. Once the deer got close enough, BAM—a shot rang out. The animal laid out, bleeding, staring numbly into the eyes of the hunter. The woman, a housewife, kneeled down beside the animal and carefully, slowly, flayed it alive, peeling back its skin, her forearms streaked with blood, which she wiped on her apron. She carried the head home, placed it in her garage to dry out. Once it was clean and ready, she hung it on her gate. A prize and a warning.

But none of that actually happened. People here would never get their hands so dirty.

"Nothing," Mar said. She pointed to a NO THRU WAY sign and a daintily decorated NO SOLICITING plaque. "Your neighbors sure put a lot of effort into telling people where not to go."

Xavier looked at Mar the way he did sometimes, his head cocked to one side, like he couldn't quite figure her out. Then, glancing around, he pointed at a NEIGHBORHOOD WATCH sign.

"Yeah, like who gets to decide who is part of this neighborhood and who needs to be watched?"

She nodded. Xavier's shoulders fell an inch down his back.

As they rounded the bend, Xavier gestured toward a house on the corner. "Well, this is it," he said. "Home sweet home."

The house was two stories high, with wide windows and

dark brown shingles. From where they stood, Mar could see all the way through the living room out to the back terrace. Even in the haze, she caught a breathtaking slice of towering pines beyond the deck.

Xavier opened the front door, unlocked. They stepped into the hall. Mar made a concerted effort to keep her jaw from dropping. The space was massive, the ceiling stretching high overhead, wooden beams cutting across it, like inside the belly of a ship. Glancing out the back windows, it felt as though they were hanging in midair. Only the trees closest in were visible, the rest hidden partly by a thin cloud of smoke. A few spindly, green-tufted branches poked through, long fingers reaching through the fog, droplets made not of water, but of ash.

Mar slipped out of her shoes so as not to track dirt onto the pristine floors. She followed Xavier up the winding staircase to his room. When she stepped inside, she broke into a laugh. She pointed at the cases of Pamplemousse LaCroix stacked under his bed.

"What? A man's gotta hydrate," Xavier said, nudging her.

Mar shoved him gently back. She moved toward the glass case above his desk, which held dozens of feathers, each with a tiny hand-scribbled label pinned underneath. She recognized the long bluish-black feather of a Steller's jay; the short, warm nutty brown of a California towhee; the rusted red of a hawk's tail. It was a tiny museum of birds' wings. It made her sad, seeing them all encased like that, instead of fluttering about in the air, or softly lining the inside of a bird's nest.

"It's nice up here," Mar said, inhaling deeply. It was the first time she'd breathed clear air in days.

"Yeah, my mom went a little overboard with the purifiers," Xavier said. He rolled his eyes and nodded at a sleek silver box in the corner of the room.

Mar thought about her dad's place. She closed all the windows at night despite the heat, to try to keep out the filthy air. She lay in bed sweating, and yet, come morning, it all still smelled just as badly of smoke. The ash particles snuck into her room some-how, scurrying through the vents, digging passages in the cracks in the walls, penetrating her lungs. Mar had done a quick online search for an air purifier, but when she saw it would cost at least two hundred dollars for a halfway decent one, she clicked out.

"Let me show you something," Xavier said. He swung his desk chair around and gestured for her to sit down. He put a large pair of headphones over her ears. "Close your eyes."

All at once, Mar was surrounded by the low buzz of insects and then, the high-pitched trill of a bird—a dozen notes petering out in rapid succession, each twee shorter than the last, until the call faded and the hum of insects resumed.

Mar slid one headphone off, smiling: "You're playing me a birdsong?"

"The California towhee," Xavier said, beaming. "I recorded their calls from the deck. I'm going to make an audio track to match up with my feather collection. It's the art project I'm planning to submit for my application to RISD. The idea is, like: nature in a box."

"Ah. Or, people could just . . . step outside," Mar said.

Xavier's grin dropped, and she quickly added: "I'm kidding. It's a cool idea. Really."

He gestured for her to put the headphones back on. Mar closed her eyes and was surrounded by the unmistakable sound of the woods—far-off twitters and, closer-in, the rapid-fire taps of a woodpecker. She opened her mouth to tell Xavier she'd fig-ured it out—that one was easy—but Xavier brought a finger to his lips, gestured for her to stay still. Eyes closed, she listened. Suddenly, from what felt like miles away, she heard an arching, melancholy cry piercing the air. Her heart seized as the mournful sound rang out again. It echoed around her, plunging her into a feeling of intense longing. Mar's eyes opened and locked with Xavier's, glittering with delight.

"Red-tailed hawk," she said.

"Isn't it amazing?"

He took the headphones back, wrapped his fingers around her hand. She pulled away.

Mar couldn't let this happen. She couldn't fall for him. She had no interest in having her attention ripped away from her studies, from her singular drive to get into college and off to something better. And also, somewhere tucked inside the folds of her resistance, she was afraid. She didn't want to replicate what she'd had a front-row seat to over the past few years: how two people, once madly in love, could slowly break each other down, make each other feel small, unworthy, until they were each just shells of their former selves, hardened and alone.

"I should probably go," Mar said, getting up to leave.

"Hold up. Next week, my mom is having that party," Xavier said hurriedly. "Maybe you could come over? Not to the party. That's at my mom's friend's place. I mean here. I haven't caught the sound of a spotted owl yet. They only come out late at night. Maybe you could help me find one?"

Mar hesitated.

"No one else will be home," Xavier added. He pushed his glasses up the bridge of his nose.

Mar swallowed. "Yeah, okay."

———

The smoke had gotten markedly worse. Firefighters in the next county over were struggling to beat back the blaze, full as the edge of Tilden Park was of dried-out bushes, crisp leaves, tall trees with bark gray from months without moisture, all ripe for burning.

Abigail cursed the air being so awful on the day her mother was set to arrive. Not very festive. She was used to this, of course: the unpredictable air quality during fire season, the occasional concern at a nearby blaze. But this fire was still miles away, not threatening any houses. It just felt like poor timing, was all.

Abigail walked through the living room, her eyes roaming over every corner, making sure it was neat. She put away stray water glasses in the dishwasher, folded sofa blankets into their wicker baskets, removed sneakers from chaotic piles at the entrance and tossed them into Xavier's closet. Small flaws she didn't usually notice magnified under the anticipation of her mother's gaze: the Persian rug faded in spots where the sun hit through the window, the deck worn down from years of scraping tables and chairs across it.

Abigail sighed. She filled a watering can and, glancing from one side to the other, poured generously into the soil beneath her bonsai. It wasn't a great look, soaking one's houseplants in the middle of a drought, but all of the smoke and heat were really drying up her Japanese red maple, and she'd be damned if she was going to let years of careful pruning go to waste.

She'd considered canceling the party if the smoke kept up, but it was a bit late for that now—the caterer was booked, all the RSVPs had come in, her mother would be arriving from New York any minute. More important, the success of the housing project depended on this event. If they hit their goal number for the night, almost all of the apartments they'd originally planned for could end up being funded. A massive win. One she badly needed.

She would just suggest to Marcia that they move the festivities inside. Nothing a few air purifiers couldn't take care of.

The doorbell rang, sending a jolt up Abigail's spine.

She opened the door to find her mother, dressed head-to-toe in black, sunglasses and all. Like she was attending a funeral. Abigail could picture her perfectly, seated in coach, gesturing at the flight attendant to bring over another miniature cabernet, casting judgmental glances at the passengers whom she'd deemed not appropriately dressed for air travel. Abigail resisted rolling her eyes.

"Ma, so glad you made it," she said, giving her mother a kiss on the cheek, taking her bag.

"I honestly can't fathom how you all live like this," Naomi said. Her gaze slowly made the rounds of the house before landing back on Abigail. "The air is just dreadful."

"It's not always like this," Abigail said. "You should see it in the spring. Everything is blooming. The whole neighborhood smells of wisteria."

Naomi humphed noncommittally and moved through the room, slowly circling around its edge like a Realtor at an appraisal. Or a hawk homing in on its prey.

"So what do you think?" Abigail asked, hoping the strain in her voice wasn't as obvious to her mother as it sounded to her. "We redid some of it since you were here last. I don't know if you remember."

"It's very nice, Abby," Naomi said, sitting on the sofa. "But you knew that."

There it was. Abigail should have expected it. Her mother's compliments always came with a backhanded slap. Even at her age, the comment stung in the way only a mother's could, seeping deep into Abigail's bones, promising to chew at her self-worth for days to come.

Abigail's childhood had been spent in a household that was quiet, financially comfortable, and harshly judgmental. Money was meant for security, not frivolity. Necessity, not enjoyment.

Her father, a reserved man, had died before Abigail turned nine. Cancer, official diagnosis. The Holocaust, her mother's. He'd been born before the war, spent his infancy in hiding in Czechoslovakia and then his childhood in Brooklyn, raised by parents haunted by the loved ones who'd been murdered and the fact that they had not. Naomi, a third-generation Brooklynite, was born to people who'd escaped a different yet similar persecution, the Russian pogroms. She was quick to vocalize her opinions, reticent to reveal her emotions. Her life had been one of sacrifice: she'd left a good job as a travel agent to raise Abigail. And then she'd been left without a husband. They got by on Abigail's father's life insurance, which Naomi spent just enough of to maintain the appearance that they were doing just fine, thank you. And Abigail understood in ways Naomi never explicitly expressed that her mother might have been someone, if she were not so swiftly made a parent and then a widow. So in a sense, Abigail understood her mother's fervent wish that she "make something of herself." And yet it didn't help it to weigh any less. A poisonous cocktail of ardent hope and lung-crushing pressure.

Abigail sighed. She turned away, fiddling with the air purifier in an attempt to hide the frustrated tears coming to her eyes.

Get it together, she admonished herself. *Barely a minute in and you're already a mess.*

A peal of laughter erupted from the hallway and Abigail turned to see Xavier and Mar strolling into the kitchen. Her body flooded with relief. Someone else to turn Naomi's attention to.

"Bubbe!" Xavier said, jogging over to hug his grandmother.

"My handsome boychik." Naomi opened her arms wide and folded Xavier into her chest.

Abigail was always in awe, and a tad jealous, at the ease Xavier had with his grandmother. She couldn't remember the last time her mother had held her like that.

"What are you two getting up to?" Naomi said, casting a not-so-generous look up and down at Mar, which Abigail hoped to God the girl didn't notice.

"Just some birdwatching club stuff," Xavier said, opening the fridge and pulling out a bottle of seltzer.

He'd announced to Abigail the other day that he no longer wanted LaCroix, only "normal" seltzer, made with a machine, no less, because that was apparently better for the environment. Abigail balked at the price of the device—$250. She smelled Mar behind all this. Still, she bought it. These were her last few months sharing a house with her son. Best not to rock the boat.

"Let me know if you kids need anything else," Abigail said. "Oh, and Xavier, keep those windows shut and the purifier on high. The air is just dreadful."

"I know," Xavier said, not bothering to hide his eye roll. He turned to leave.

"I was thinking maybe we could go up to Tahoe next weekend," Abigail said, trying to keep them in the room a little longer. "Get away from all the smoke. You know how awful it is for Mama's asthma."

"Climate refugees," Mar said, under her breath.

"What was that?"

Mar turned as though surprised at being overheard. "Oh, nothing. I just said, 'climate refugees.' You know, people displaced by natural disasters."

"Oh, I don't know that I would call us *refugees*." Abigail half laughed, half scoffed, glancing at her mother, whose lips were pursed.

"No, obviously not," the girl said pensively. "More like . . . climate expats."

Xavier frowned. "Yeah, I'm not going to Tahoe, Mom," he said, marching upstairs.

"All right. It was just a thought," Abigail said to their backs.

Climate expats. She wasn't sure what the girl meant by it, but she knew she didn't like it.

"Rather than toying around with girls, shouldn't my grandson be working on his college applications?" Naomi said once the kids were out of earshot.

Abigail had actually been wondering the same thing. They were only a couple months shy of the deadline, and she had no idea where Xavier was with his essays. But that realization alone—that she'd had the same nagging thought as her mother—put Abigail firmly off the idea of asking him.

"It's fine, Ma. He's got it taken care of."

With Xavier, Abigail had tried a different approach than her mother had in raising her. She'd been careful to never utter anything close to *make something of yourself.* Instead, Abigail told her son, "You can be whoever you want to be," when she tucked him in at night. "I love you just the way you are," when she scrubbed tear-free shampoo through his locks at bath time.

Even so, she recognized that children needed *some* guidance to not feel completely unmoored. But Xavier wouldn't let his mothers even glance at his essays. Over the last few weeks, he'd begun railing against parents who wrote their kids' college applications, calling it "elite opportunity hoarding." (Abigail smelled Mar in that one, too.) She didn't want to *write* the damn thing. Just . . . provide some edits. Was it so bad to want to give her son the same edge every other kid at his school had? Xavier had no idea how cutthroat admissions had gotten.

Naomi installed herself on the sofa and pulled out a *Vanity Fair* from her full-to-bursting handbag. Flopping the magazine open in her lap, she rhythmically licked a finger and flicked through it, humming occasional disapproval at one model or another before turning to the next spread. Abigail might as well not even be there.

Her phone vibrated, and she looked at the screen: REMINDER: BE GRATEFUL. She grunted. She had set the alarm months ago at the recommendation of her therapist, after a particularly difficult session in which she'd wondered if she was doing enough with her life, contributing enough to the world—making something of herself, in short. Her therapist recommended she "be a little less meta" and write down three things she was grateful for each day. For this, she paid the woman $260 a session.

"I *am* grateful," Abigail muttered to her phone. She needed to get out of the house.

"You know what, Ma? I'm going to let you settle in here," Abigail said, moving toward the door. "I laid out some towels on your bed in the guest room upstairs."

Naomi looked up, as though annoyed at being interrupted.

"I'm just heading to the food bank for my usual volunteer shift—wouldn't want to leave them helpless." Abigail chuckled.

"I can occupy myself, you know," Naomi said.

"I know you can, Ma," Abigail said. "Okay. Well, I'm off."

Her mother turned back to her magazine.

Abigail grabbed her tote and walked out the door. She got into the Subaru only to find it was almost out of gas. *Fuck.* She gripped the steering wheel. *Inhale, exhale.* Fine. She'd just take Taylor's car. She didn't love the idea of rolling up to the community center in the BMW, but she'd just park a few blocks away and walk over.

———

Across town, past the flowers of the Berkeley Rose Garden emanating a pungent scent as they wilted in the smoky heat, beyond the eight exhaust-filled lanes of the 101, inside the van parked at the edge of the water, Willow sat up, blinking wildly, her eyes stinging. The hint of a headache she'd woken up to had bloomed into a full-fledged migraine. Whenever she swallowed, she could feel the saliva burning as it slid down her throat. The air inside the van was thick with smoke, a layer of white ash coating the windows, rendering the light seeping through a macabre glow.

Willow started the car, flicking on the wipers to scrape off the gray film. *Fuck.* They were nearly out of gas. She'd have to walk to the community center. They'd fill up again once Sunny got his paycheck.

At the food bank, the air wasn't all that much clearer, but the vaulted ceilings and fans at least gave some sense of circulation. Willow went to the back office to drop Aso off with Jo, who had a soft spot for old pit bulls and liked to sneak the dog treats under their desk.

"Hello, little fart monster," Jo said, reaching for the jar of beef nibs. They turned up the radio: "Listen to this."

A gravelly voice came through the old boom box: "I've been fighting fires for over two decades now. I've never seen a fire so wild."

The flames reached dozens of feet into the air in some places, the firefighter said. The blaze had torn through the ancient redwoods and eucalyptus groves of Wildcat Canyon, licked at the edges of Tilden Park. In some places, it was spreading at the rate of a football field per minute.

"Jesus," Willow said.

"Yeah. California for you—can't live here, can't live anywhere else."

Then Jo grinned incomprehensibly. "Speaking of living here . . ." They turned their computer screen to face Willow. "Guess who was approved for one of the apartments in that new building going up on the west side!"

Willow froze. "No." She shook her head. "Shut up."

"Don't get too excited," Jo said. "It's not official yet, so don't let anyone know I told you—besides Sunny, of course. They're still waiting on some final funding to come through. But I know the person planning the fundraiser for it, and she seems confident it'll pan out. I just couldn't help telling you. I know how huge this would be for you guys."

Willow gripped the back of the chair in front of her, steadying herself.

An apartment. All their own.

The building wouldn't be available to move into for another few weeks, Jo said, likely sometime in November. And there was still this fundraising event they were counting on. But Willow barely heard them.

She was thinking of the pictures she'd seen of the apartments online. The description that she'd read over and over, back when they'd applied: a kitchen with a full-size fridge. A bathtub big enough to sink both her chest and her knees into at once.

She couldn't wait to tell Sunny. She'd break the news in person. She wanted to see the look on his face. To kiss the disbelief from his eyes and tell him that, contrary to his conviction that life was mostly shit that you had to wade through, things could actually be good, sometimes.

"Holy shit," she said.

"Amen to that." Jo turned back to their computer, smiling. They stroked Aso as the dog settled into a ball at their feet.

Willow lugged a box of canned soup into the dining hall, almost bumping into a woman who was standing at the volunteer tables. Her short, dark hair was stylishly swept back from her face. She was wearing white khakis, which Willow wondered at the wisdom of, given the coat of dust and ash on every surface. The woman looked vaguely familiar.

"Hello!" The woman extended her hand. "I don't think

we've met yet. I'm Abigail, a volunteer here. Can I help you with those?"

"Sure," Willow said, handing her a box. "There are more in the back, for the evening rush."

Abigail put down her tote, which had GIVE A SHIT, DON'T EAT MEAT written across it. It dawned on Willow where she'd seen her before. She was the woman from outside the bakery. The one who'd knocked over her cup and handed her a ten-dollar bill. Willow felt a twinge of discomfort. She wasn't going to say anything. Clearly, Abigail had no idea who she was.

They doled out bags filled with cereal bars, apples, and canned vegetables, and Abigail talked Willow's ear off. She'd grown up in New York, apparently, but the Brooklyn of today was nothing like when she was a kid, all "hipsters on electric bikes drinking eight-dollar lattes." She'd been in California for decades now, and "you couldn't drag me back east if you tried," she said, laughing oddly.

"So are you from here?" Abigail asked, when Willow didn't respond.

"Not too far. Tahoe." Willow didn't like making small talk, especially about her childhood, but she didn't want to be rude. And today, she was in a good mood.

"Oh my, how gorgeous," Abigail said, her eyes alight. "We try to spend a few weekends there each summer. I bet you miss the lake on days like this. The water so clear you can see your toes when you're in chest-deep."

Willow conjured the feeling of the lake's cool ripples on her legs. How the tall pines made her feel small as she walked along the forest floor, dry needles softly snapping underfoot. She did miss it.

"I don't know why you would ever leave such a heavenly place," Abigail said dreamily.

A shiver ran down Willow's spine. She shut her eyes and saw the garish green and pink tiles of the bathroom walls, felt his belly pressing into her ribs, her spine digging into the cold, hard floor, his weight suffocating her. She twisted away as his hairy hands crept determinedly up her shorts. But he only pulled her in closer, grinning as he told her that he'd seen how she looked at him all those years, knew this was what she wanted. Afterward, when he tossed her clothes over to her—"Get dressed before your mother sees you like this," almost casual—Willow scraped the recesses of her mind, trying to remember if she had said "no" in so many words. She could have sworn she had, but then again, she wasn't sure if she had said anything at all. Not that it mattered at this point. As Willow washed her hands and scrubbed her face, rinsed the inside of her mouth with fistfuls of water, avoided her reflection in the mirror, slipped her shorts tenderly back on, she listened to the sounds of the television, turned back on in the living room. The evening news, just like any other night. When she came out of the bathroom, her face swollen red with tears, her footsteps off-kilter, it was her mother's glare that took Willow's breath right out of her. Her mother gave the same response she had all the times before, when Willow's stepdad had looked at her with his sideways, drunken grin and said, "Aren't you a sight for sore eyes?" Her mother's eyes narrowed. "Don't go making trouble for me now."

"Yeah, I prefer the Bay," Willow said to Abigail, shoving a pack of canned corn deep into a bag. "Small towns can get claustrophobic."

"I could see that," Abigail said, apparently unbothered by Willow's long pause.

Abigail kept up her end of a largely one-way conversation, explaining her fervent dislike of San Francisco: "That cold wind, and the fog! You might as well live in London." (Willow wondered if she'd ever felt how the fog could penetrate a sleeping bag at night, digging its cold moisture into your bones.) Abigail worried about her son applying to college: "He's determined to go to this art school out east, but the competition is so fierce these days, it's almost unfair, honestly." Most of all, she was agitated about the climate: "All this smoke, year after year, it makes you wonder if the Bay will even be livable in a couple of decades." (Willow wondered if Abigail thought the Bay was livable now.)

But for all her quiet judgments, Willow took a liking to the woman. She appreciated her persistent friendliness. It got lonely spending her days with Aso while Sunny worked. She could use a friend.

"Do you live around here?" Willow asked.

"Not too far," Abigail said. "We're just up the hill, a few blocks from the Rose Garden. I don't know if you know it. Actually, this is a wretched time of year to see it. You should check it out in June, when the blooms come in. It's pure magic. You?"

"We're by the water," Willow said. "Our van is parked on West Frontage Road, near the marina?"

Willow saw the surprise register on Abigail's face.

"The marina's lovely," Abigail said slowly. Then her face hardened, resolute. "You know, the homelessness crisis really is out of control. I work in affordable housing, so I understand how impossible it is for people to get by around here."

Willow nodded. True enough.

Abigail turned to her, her eyes alight, one hand pressed into Willow's forearm. "You know what? We're throwing a party this weekend, at a friend's," she said excitedly.

Willow smiled. She couldn't remember the last time she'd been invited to a party, other than the cookout the community center threw each summer.

"Well, actually, it's my birthday party," Abigail said. "But it's also going to be a fundraiser for the new building going up on the west side. Anyhow, it just occurred to me: Would you be interested in working it?"

Willow felt a hollow expanding in her chest. Oh. She wasn't being invited to the party; she was being asked to serve the guests. At an event raising funds for tenants of the new building. In other words, for her. "Um, I'm not sure . . ."

"We could really use the help. It'll just be basic stuff, bringing out hors d'oeuvres and drinks, a little cleanup afterward," Abigail said quickly. "We'd pay you, of course."

Willow paused. She could certainly use the money. The rent would be low at the new place, but it wasn't nothing. And maybe this would turn up other opportunities down the road. She'd worked in restaurants before. It could be a way back to steady work, slowly but surely, gig by gig.

"I guess that would be okay," Willow said.

"Oh, I'm so glad." Abigail turned back to fill the next bag, a relieved smile softening her lips.

———

On the west side of the city, in a neighborhood along the shore, with small, worn-down houses tucked between block-long industrial buildings and new luxury condos being built up along a commercial strip, Mar, Xavier, and Lena trudged through the smoky heat, pushing a cart of bird feed and gallons of water.

With the smoke thickening, Xavier had the idea to put out fresh food for migratory birds. The birdwatching club raised money from the PTA (i.e., Xavier asked his moms for cash) so they could feed the golden-crowned sparrows, black-throated blue warblers, and orange-breasted thrush that usually found respite along the Bay's wetlands on their southbound routes, but were struggling to rest lately, exhausted and parched as they tried to evade the mounting heat, smoke, and flames. Donning masks that Ms. Plummer insisted they wear, the teens searched for parklets with birdbaths to fill, stray branches to dangle feeders from.

"This smoke is fucked," Lena said, reaching up into a live oak tree. She wrapped a wire around its low-hanging arms and shoved a seed block between the feeder's bars for desperate birds to peck at.

"Yeah, these fires are fucked," Mar echoed.

As they walked through the nearly empty streets, Mar thought of how the smoke made it impossible to keep her bedroom windows open, but the heat made it torturous to keep them shut.

They passed a construction site surrounded by a chain-link fence. A gleaming, six-story building stood proudly in its center. A large sign read: FOR LEASE: 1-BD, 2-BD, 3-BD—AVAILABLE THIS FALL.

"You know, there are bodies buried under there," Lena said.

Mar froze. She frowned skeptically. "What do you mean?"

Lena pointed at hand-painted cloth banners that hung along the outside of the fence: SAVE THE SHELLMOUND. PROTECT IN-DIGENOUS SACRED SITES.

"The land they built this on was actually an ancestral burial ground for Ohlone people," Lena said. She curled her purple-and-red-painted fingernails through the chain-link, gripping it. "My family's Ohlone. My mom told me how some developer dug all this up to build an apartment complex. The city agreed, ignoring activists' demands that they return the land to our tribe."

Xavier shifted uncomfortably from one foot to the other.

After a beat, he said, "I think my mom helped negotiate that deal. Apparently, a bunch of the apartments are going to low-income housing? She said it's supposed to be good, to help the homeless."

Lena snorted. "You can have both, you know. Build afford-able housing and not wreck the sacred sites of the people whose land you stole."

Xavier stared at the asphalt and said nothing.

Lena walked on. "You know Indigenous communities back in the day used to do prescribed burns? Small, controlled fires to prevent bigger ones, to allow for plants and crops to regrow."

"They lit fires on purpose?" Mar asked, following her.

"Mhmm. And if the colonizers hadn't come and wrecked ev-erything with their diseases and mass murder and shit—and ig-nored Native practices—maybe it wouldn't all be this way now."

Lena gestured vaguely at the ash-tinged air. Her mother used to tell her stories of what their hometown looked like hundreds of years ago, how Berkeley was full of trees and fields, forests climb-ing up into the hills, home to grizzly bears and mountain lions. And how after the Spaniards came, they started logging old-growth trees, turning vast stretches of the shoreline into lumberyards.

Mar pictured the ancient redwoods she camped under every summer being chopped down and shipped off, their regal trunks turned into soulless walls, beams, and tables.

She pulled a feeder from the cart. She twisted its thin metal wire around the topmost link of the fence. The people laid there to rest likely had enough of all the noise of construction. They might find some comfort in listening to the sounds of a mourning dove's coo or a blackbird's chirp.

Xavier trailed behind, kneeling down to read the signs that activists had lined up along the fence.

Lena nudged Mar: "So what's up with you two?"

Mar shrugged noncommittally.

"Don't think I don't see how y'all are together," Lena insisted.

"I mean, I *like* him, obviously, as a friend," Mar said. "It's just . . ."

She flashed back to the day her mom found out her dad was cheating. She'd never seen her so angry. She could still hear the crash of dishes against the tiled kitchen floor. "Ves eso?" her mom yelled, while her dad stood mutely. "Eso es lo que le has hecho a mi corazón." Mar imagined her mom's heart splayed out on the floor, exploded into a thousand bloody, pulsing pieces.

"He's one of my only friends here. I'm not trying to mess that up," Mar said. "And sometimes, good things go to shit for no reason."

"True," Lena said, threading her arm through Mar's. "But you know, he's actually *not* your only friend here—ahem. And also, you could maybe try to just . . . loosen up, and live a little?"

Mar laughed. Loosen up. Live a little. Easier said than done.

When Xavier caught up with them, he took the cart from Lena, pushing it forward. He turned to Mar, smiling mischievously. "Hop in."

"I don't know about that," Mar said.

She glanced at Lena, who cocked her eyebrow.

Mar climbed into the plastic bed, kneeling between the remaining jugs of water. Xavier pushed the cart slowly at first, then picked up speed, running down the sidewalk. The cart careened from side to side. Mar laughed, releasing an elated scream. The breeze generated as they sped down the street cooled her face. She closed her eyes. Loosening.

"Stop!" Lena yelled.

They screeched to a halt. Just feet ahead, a woman sat on the ground with her back against a building. A pit bull lay at her side. A sign propped in front of them read: ANYTHING HELPS. The woman's shirt was pulled up over her mouth in what couldn't have been a very effective barrier against the smoke.

Xavier reached into the cart. One by one, he hauled the remaining water jugs out and deposited them at the woman's feet.

She nodded her thanks, her eyes crinkling at the corners above her makeshift mask.

As they walked on, Lena said quietly: "Weren't we supposed to use your moms' money for bird stuff only?"

Xavier shrugged. "You gonna tell?"

Lena puffed air skeptically from her lips. "Hell no."

Mar placed one hand on the cart. When Xavier moved his fingers to overlap hers, she didn't pull away.

————

In the dark of night, the fire curled its way through the rolling acres of Tilden Park, climbing up cypresses, cracking the thin trunks of tall pines, splitting long branches of sequoia, shriveling leaves into dust. Some redwoods groaned in protest; a few maples snapped as they fell to the forest floor. Most of the trees stayed standing, gathering the strength of their hundreds of years, holding steady down to their roots as the flames enveloped them, ran through them, left stains like a funeral dress on their bark.

————

Sunny started awake. It was pitch black and a loud banging was coming from the side of the van.

"Police!" a deep voice barked.

He looked up from the bed in the back of the car and saw a light beaming through the windshield.

"One second!" Sunny said loudly. As he adjusted to the dark he could see the whites of Willow's eyes beside him, popped wide in fear. "It's okay," he whispered.

The pounding got louder. "Step out of your vehicle!" the voice barked. "This is unlawful overnight parking."

Sunny scrambled toward the van doors. Placing one hand on the latch and the other up in the air, he paused and then said as loudly and clearly as he could: "I'm coming out. Please don't shoot."

The last time he'd held his hands up like this, his heart beating loudly against his chest, he was seventeen, staring out the driver's-side window of his friend's car. Two cops stared back at him, their guns drawn. He'd been waiting for his friends to come out of the gas station convenience store. They were supposed to be quick—they'd promised. In and out. They'd get the cash from the register, and nobody would get hurt. All Sunny had to do was wait, and keep his foot near the gas for the moment they came running out. But the minutes ticked by and they didn't emerge, and Sunny couldn't see past the stacks of toilet paper and Cheerios in the window to what was happening inside. Later, in the cold interrogation room at the police station, alone and shivering after hours of a cop with a goatee and bad breath grilling him, all Sunny could think about was what his father would say. Under the harsh neon lights, as Goatee asked why they'd shot the cashier (he didn't know; he wasn't there) and how long they'd planned this (they hadn't, or at least *he* hadn't—he'd just come along for the ride), his father's voice said: "Nadismaya ako sayo." His dad spoke Tagalog when he was angry, which was more and more often those days. "I'm disappointed in you." Years later, when Sunny got out of prison, he took the two hundred dollars the state gave him and bought a one-way ticket to San Francisco. He called home only once, to tell his mother not to worry, but he wasn't coming back. "You're better off without me," Sunny said, crying, listening to his mother's sharp sobs. He waited a beat to see if his father would say anything. When he didn't, Sunny hung up.

Staring into the glare of the cop's flashlight, Sunny stepped gingerly out of the van, his hands held high.

"You alone in that vehicle?" the officer said, louder than necessary given they were only a few feet apart.

When he shined the beam into the back of the van, Sunny saw the man's face for the first time. He was Asian, too. And he had one hand poised on his holster.

With a tremble in his voice, Sunny told the officer that his girlfriend was still in the van. Willow climbed out, her eyes squinting, Sunny's Fugees T-shirt barely reaching the tops of her bare thighs. Aso growled, and Willow quickly hushed him.

"It's okay, Officer," Willow said. She spoke in a register Sunny had heard her use with law enforcement before: high-pitched and soft, her words slow and deliberate. He wondered who she'd first learned to use that voice with, to appease.

"We'll head right out," she said. "No problem."

The cop let them go with a fine and a promise never to park overnight there again.

As the van pulled away, the time flickered on the dashboard: one a.m. His hands still shaking, Sunny drove aimlessly through the streets, his heart thumping in his chest, his mind unable to land on a good spot to park to get some sleep.

"Go up into the hills," Willow said, her hand on his thigh, steadying him. "That way at least we'll be close to that party for my job. We can figure out where to go after that."

Only a few more weeks, Sunny thought. That's what Willow had said when she broke the news to him, beaming. Then they'd move into their new place. Their own actual apartment. He still couldn't believe it. He couldn't picture the day that they would walk in and close the door and sit in the quiet. They'd go to sleep and not have to worry about being woken up in the night. They'd have somewhere to rest at any time of day. No one could say they had to leave, they couldn't be there, they had to exist elsewhere, or preferably disappear altogether.

A red light flashed on the dash: they were nearly out of gas. *Fuck*. He'd deal with that later.

When they finally pulled into a quiet, residential street across from the Rose Garden, Sunny comforted himself with the thought that the cops likely wouldn't come looking to ticket anyone here. Too fancy.

He crawled into the back of the van and plopped down on the mattress beside Willow. He tucked his head into the crook of her arm, inhaling her smell and listening to the sound of an owl hooting nearby. *We're safe*, he repeated to himself, trying to fall back asleep. *We survived.*

Later that day, after missing work and being too exhausted to care, Sunny sat in the yellowed grass of Codornices Park, waiting for Willow to emerge from the van. He was growing light-headed from all the smoke, but he didn't want to rush her. He wondered if it was such a good idea to be parked up here, with the fire growing nearby. But he also knew how much working this event meant to her. He couldn't remember the last time she'd had a paying job. He didn't want to mess that up.

The door opened and Willow peeked her head out. "Ready?" she asked shyly.

She stepped out onto the sidewalk. Her long hair was loose, flowing around her shoulders instead of in her usual ponytail. She was wearing a long, strappy green dress with aqua-blue waves shimmering down to her ankles. Sunny felt his breath catch in his throat.

It had been years since he'd seen that dress. It was the one she wore the day they got married, barefoot on the beach. It settled differently on her body now. Her breasts filled out the top, and her hips gave the fabric a new stretch, like this was how it was always meant to fit, a mermaid's second skin.

"Is it too much?" Willow asked, blushing and retreating back toward the van. "It's too much, isn't it?"

Sunny shook his head. "No, it's perfect. You're perfect."

He remembered all the times that they'd moved—first from a tent to a shelter, then to a friend's couch, then the van. Each time he'd begged her to get rid of the dress, among a host of other unnecessary items occupying their preciously little space. He was glad she hadn't listened to him.

Sunny felt an unfamiliar tingle running through his body. With the apartment coming and Willow's gig at the party, maybe their luck was finally turning. Maybe, possibly, unfathomably, life could actually go their way.

———

Standing outside the house, Camila took in the stark white façade and wondered how much work the gardener had put into getting the vines to circle so neatly up each of the columns like that. She estimated that their house in San Jose would probably fit into one-third of the left wing of this place.

Despite the thick smoke giving the sky an eerie orange glow, Camila waited for Gabriel to arrive before going in. She'd been reluctant to come, partly because of all the smoke and partly because it felt weird to show up as a "couple" to an event for the first time since the divorce. But Gabriel convinced her it was worth getting to know the parents at Mar's school.

"Guapa," she heard behind her. Camila spun around to see Gabriel walking over in a formfitting suit. She had to admit, he looked good.

He leaned in to give Camila a peck on the cheek. She nodded toward the house.

"You think those columns hold up anything other than the owners' fragile egos?"

Gabriel laughed. He put his hand to the small of her back as they walked up the front steps.

Abigail answered the door as soon as they rang, almost as though she'd been waiting on the other side.

"Happy birthday!" Gabriel said, handing her a bottle. "Thank you again for inviting us."

"Oh, you shouldn't have," Abigail said, taking the bottle and ushering them into the room.

There were a few dozen people dotted throughout the ample space. The walls were an aggressive white, the art hanging on them dripped with abstract black lines and red splashes. Camila found it all fairly boring. A handful of servers rotated through the room with trays of food. Lauryn Hill played in the background.

"The air is nice in here," Camila said to Abigail. "You'd almost forget there was a fire nearby."

Gabriel shot Camila a warning glance. She pretended not to notice.

"We have half a dozen purifiers going," Abigail said. "But if Californians stopped making plans because of the smoke, we wouldn't go anywhere from August to December, right?"

Gabriel chuckled. Camila offered a tight smile.

"Thank you for this," Abigail said, frowning and turning back toward the bottle. "What is it?"

"Aguardiente. An Ecuadorian liquor," Gabriel said.

"It's named for how it burns your throat," Camila added.

"How fun!" Abigail said. "Is that where you're from— Ecuador?"

"Yes, my family is from a small mountain town outside Quito," Gabriel said.

"I'm from Fresno," Camila said, looking toward the bar at the back of the room.

Camila felt Gabriel's fingers dig into her back where his hand had been resting.

"You know, I spent some time in Latin America myself," Abigail said. "Back in my college years, I volunteered for a summer in Nicaragua. Beautiful place. Beautiful people."

"Ah, I've never been," Gabriel said, smiling and glancing at Camila, silently urging her to rejoin the conversation. She flicked his hand away from her back.

"I didn't learn all that much while I was there, pero hablo un poco de español," Abigail said, giggling.

"Ah, qué bien!"

Abigail led them over to a man in a crisp white shirt and stiff khakis standing by the buffet. "Brice! I want to introduce you to my new friends, Gabriel and Camila. Their daughter, Mar, goes to Berkeley High. She's a good friend of Xavier's. Spunky girl."

Camila smiled tightly.

"Brice's son just graduated last year," Abigail said. "He's at Stanford now. Only an hour's drive away—every parent's dream!"

The man grinned like he was the one who'd gotten into Stanford. He wiped his greasy fingers on a cocktail napkin and offered up his hand to shake. "I just peeked at the auction table," he said, winking at Abigail. "It looks like our place up in Sea Ranch is gathering some nice bids."

"Oh, you're too kind for offering that up," Abigail said. "Anyhoo, I'll leave you all to chat. I'm off to greet the newcomers. Enjoy!" Her kaftan swayed as she made her way back toward the entrance.

"Nice to meet you," Gabriel said. "So do you spend much time up in Sea Ranch? I've never been myself."

Camila recognized Gabriel's tone as the one he used when speaking to colleagues, or to the host at a fancy restaurant. Polite, overly friendly. Deferential. It drove her mad.

Brice was telling Gabriel that he really ought to drive up the Sonoma Coast. The views along Highway 1 were sublime. Oh, and the oysters in Bodega Bay. Exquisite. Anyway, wasn't it wonderful that Abigail was throwing this fundraiser, on her birthday of all times? So generous. But that's the kind of people they'd find in the Berkeley High community. People who cared.

"Well, it does seem a bit off, no?" Camila cut in. She couldn't help herself. "This is all to raise money for people to afford living in a new development in the heart of the city, right? And doesn't it strike you as a bit messed up that someone's housing—a basic human right, after all—would depend on a bunch of us gathered in this air-purified room, deciding how much to put toward, say, a week on someone's yacht in Ibiza next summer?"

Gabriel stiffened.

"Well, I'm not sure how else you would propose—" Brice said, his already-thin lips pinched into an impossibly tight line.

"Taxes. On the rich," Camila said. "Public funding."

The man scoffed, and she couldn't tell if he was laughing or choking on the mini-quiche he'd grabbed from a passing tray and shoved in his mouth. He mumbled something about "certainly paying enough to Uncle Sam" and that you only needed to look at the sorry state of the roads, never mind public schools, not to mention the mentally ill roaming the streets, to wonder what the government did with it all.

Camila turned to Gabriel. She waited.

Back in grad school, when she first fell in love with him, he debated professors with a furious passion, arguing that our failing schools were a product of a broken system, a sign that we needed more, not less, public investment in the commons.

A drop of sweat gathered and fell slowly from Gabriel's temple to his jaw.

He cleared his throat, shifted from one foot to the other. Then he looked at Brice. "You're telling me!" he said. He chuckled. Brice smiled.

Camila couldn't believe it. And also, she could.

She didn't feel angry. It was worse than that. She was tired. A bone-deep exhaustion. "I'm going to grab a drink," she said. And she walked off.

As she moved through the crowd to the bar, she could hear Gabriel maneuvering painstakingly behind her, uttering a lot of *excuse me*s and *pardon me*s. She ordered a tall glass of champagne, took a long gulp, and dropped a fistful of bills into the tip jar.

"Porque te estas portando así?" Gabriel asked in a hushed tone as he sidled up to her.

"Not this." Camila turned to glare at Gabriel, her eyes ablaze. "Is this what you were picturing, when you were pushing so hard for Mar to come live with you? For our daughter to be surrounded by people like this? Have all this money rub off on her somehow? Did you not think all the pretension might, too?"

They had spent months in heated phone calls last year, hourslong arguments, with Gabriel pleading for Camila to let Mar live with him for her senior year, and Camila saying there was no way in hell. He argued that Berkeley High had a better reputation with colleges and universities, that this was what was best for Mar. She insisted that San Jose High had done just fine by their daughter so far. In the end, Gabriel played his trump card: he'd done everything she'd asked, after she got the house and full custody in the divorce—he'd found a nice place, in a good neighborhood, where Mar had her own room. Couldn't she just give him this one thing? And to her own surprise, she'd relented. Maybe he was right; maybe this was a chance to give their daughter the best shot at a good life. And maybe, also, she was sick of saying no to him, of always being the one who made the decisions. (And perhaps, quietly, she still felt something for him. She still felt the desire to soften toward him. To give him a chance to lead.) But now, standing in this airless room with these people, she remembered why she said no to Gabriel. It wasn't because she was hard or cold or stubborn. It was because she was right.

"No estás cansada de siempre ver lo peor en la gente?" Gabriel asked, making the calculation that not a lot of people here likely spoke Spanish.

"Aren't *you* tired of caring more about other people's comfort than your own dignity?" Camila shot back, not bothering to change from English.

Gabriel shook his head. "No puede ser, Camila. I can't deal with you when you're like this."

Camila's eyebrows shot up. "Perdóname, pero if I remember correctly, we ended things because *I* couldn't deal with *you* and your wandering pene."

"And why do you think I 'wandered,' eh?" Gabriel said under his breath, looking around. "You ever think maybe it was because you don't give me an inch? Nothing I do is ever good enough."

Camila sighed, a breath that came from the depths of her stomach and lodged in her chest. She regretted coming here. She didn't know why she thought it might be different this time, between them. She knocked her drink back. The alcohol here was good; she'd give them that.

———

Abigail was pleased enough with the turnout. It was a shame they'd had to move the party indoors—the whole point of Marcia's was the view. But people seemed to be having a good time.

Her eyes flitted over the room. The Hassans were there, which she hoped meant that they would be inviting her and Taylor to their annual winter gala later this year. Mar's parents were commandeering the bar, appearing to have a very vivid conversation—one that might be too lively, in fact, to have in public, given how wildly Camila was gesticulating.

At least they were talking to each other. Abigail's gaze landed on her wife, at the other end of the room. Taylor was looking out the window, into the thick wall of smoke. Abigail wanted to walk over, but she also felt oddly shy, not knowing if Taylor would want her there. These days it felt like everything she did irked her wife. Abigail responded by simply trying to do less, *be* less, tiptoeing around Taylor to avoid the sting of her rejection. Most days, this meant that she felt as invisible as old wallpaper, once carefully selected, excitedly applied, and then over the years, yellowing, peeling at the edges. And today it meant that on her birthday, in a room full of people there to celebrate her, her son was nowhere in sight and her wife was staring into a smoky abyss.

Abigail steeled herself and walked over. "I'm sweating up a storm here," she said to Taylor. "I can't tell if it's my hot flashes or the nerves of hosting."

Taylor turned to Abigail, considering her. "I guess only you could know that."

Abigail watched her wife's eyebrows knit together—in what: Pity? Boredom?

"I wish we could trade bodies for a day," Abigail said softly.

Taylor chuckled at the familiar line. It was one Abigail used to say often when they first started dating. She'd said it jokingly, but meant it viscerally. She had wanted to be under Taylor's skin, to know her very insides, the intimacy of what it felt like to *be* her. Abigail didn't want to miss out on even a fraction of a molecule of the woman she was falling so desperately in love with it almost hurt. But now the phrase came from an altogether different place. Abigail wanted to trade bodies so that Taylor would know what it felt like to be in *her* skin. To feel her insomnia, which Taylor lost patience with long ago, sleeping in the guest room so as not to be disturbed by Abigail's tossing and turning at ungodly hours. Her backaches, which Taylor dismissed with a vague suggestion to "go see a chiropractor already." Abigail wanted to be seen. Not in the way longtime partners tended to see each other, like they'd already figured each other out, knew everything there was to know about the other. She wanted her wife to light up with that old curiosity, to delight in discovering new sides to her, to recognize how she'd grown over the years, see who she was still striving to become.

Taylor looked past Abigail and nodded to the other end of the room. "Your mother is strategically positioned, as ever. You should spend some time with her, no? She did come all this way."

Abigail turned to see Naomi standing by the door to the kitchen, picking off the best hors d'oeuvres from the waiters' trays before they circulated into the room. She sighed and walked over.

"Ma, how are you holding up?" Abigail said, as her mother nabbed a piece of California roll. "I hope it's not too hot for you. Marcia has the air conditioner on blast."

"Hot, here? You've clearly forgotten August in New York."

Abigail chose to ignore the jab. "So, work's been going well these days," Abigail said, grasping for another topic of conversation. "If we collect all the donations I'm hoping for tonight, we'll be able to convert a solid portion of this new development to low-income housing. No easy feat around here."

Abigail paused, awaiting her mother's congratulations. The

truth was, she wasn't sure if they'd be able to raise enough money. The corporate developer wasn't budging much. So far, the units they'd gotten them to agree to price below market hovered around 10 percent, and even those were probably less *low*-income and more middle-income at this point. But she was hopeful that after tonight, they'd get a few more units subsidized. Frankly, anything that wasn't set at the exorbitant rates people were willing to pay these days would be a win. There was only so much one could do in the face of gentrification, Abigail thought. It was about working to slow the inevitable. Realistically, there was no stopping it altogether.

"I haven't seen my grandson. Where is Xavier?" Naomi said.

Abigail sighed. "You know what, I'll go check the kitchen." She walked off, grateful for an excuse to leave behind the sting of her mother's indifference.

———

Standing in a corner of the room, Willow watched the party-goers mill about, a tank of sharks. Precariously balancing a tray of quiches in her palm, she tried to tell herself that this job wasn't so hard. In fact, it wasn't much different from panhandling: People looked through her as though she weren't even there. They grabbed items off her tray, dropped crumpled, saliva-stained napkins into the glasses of wine she was bringing to other guests.

Gathering the courage to circulate with another round, Willow adjusted the white blouse and black slacks Abigail had lent her. She'd asked Willow to change as soon as she arrived, deeming her green dress "not entirely appropriate" for a server.

The room was filling up, sending Willow's pulse racing. *Calm down*, she thought. *There aren't that many people here. No one is smothering you. You need this job.*

Two people came over. They pulled small, eggy bites from her tray.

"Oh, Rachid!" the woman said. Willow watched her bring a cheesy fingerful to her mouth. Willow silently hoped a chunk would make its way onto her front, leave a stain on her stark white dress. "Lovely to see you here. Of course, I'm not surprised."

The man smiled graciously. He wore a tie-dyed shirt and flip-flops, like he couldn't be bothered to dress up for the occasion. He hovered beside Willow, pursing his lips, taking his time to decide which quiche looked most delectable.

"Have you seen the building they're raising money for? It's smack-dab on the water," the woman said. "Pretty swanky, if you ask me."

"I know," Rachid said. "I heard they're selecting tenants from the food bank Abigail volunteers at. I hope they're vetting people properly. If I was paying an arm and a leg for a bay view, I sure wouldn't want neighbors with, you know, drug problems or whatnot."

Willow felt her palms sweat, her breath come in shallow bursts. She kept a polite smile glued to her lips, hoping it didn't betray her fury. Her humiliation.

These people didn't know her. They didn't know Sunny. If they were so keen on vetting people, they should try drug testing the assholes who came through Tahoe every summer, getting high off their minds, crashing boat rentals into the piers. Of course, they didn't mind that kind of drug user so much. That kind they could forgive. The ones who reminded them of themselves, who received the benefit of the doubt, got second tries, and third ones—do-over after do-over.

As soon as they stepped away, Willow stumbled back toward the kitchen.

She placed the tray on the counter and looked out the window. *Breathe, Willow. Just breathe.*

The smoke outside was backlit by a strange orange glow. It pulsed and waned in the distance.

Maybe it was the sun setting. Maybe not.

"Thank God."

Willow spun around to see Abigail come into the kitchen and collapse onto a stool.

"A little peace and quiet."

Willow wasn't sure what to say. Wasn't this her party?

"That glow in the sky," Willow said. "Do you feel like it's coming closer?"

Abigail glanced briefly out the window. She took a bottle of wine from the counter and emptied it into her glass.

Willow hesitated. "Maybe we should warn folks, you know? With that fire nearby. Or cut the party short?"

"Oh no." Abigail chuckled, knocking the contents of the glass back in two gulps. "Officials haven't even put out an evacuation *warning*, let alone a mandatory evac. We'll be fine."

Willow looked back outside. The edges of the orange haze were expanding.

"There's a cake in the fridge," Abigail said. "Would you mind bringing it out a few minutes after I step back in? And stick some candles in it, from that drawer. Five should be plenty."

Willow nodded slowly. Then, a last attempt: "I do wonder if maybe people should just move their cars out from the front of the house. So they're not all crowding the driveway?"

"Now that would really be hell, trying to rally this bunch to figure out whose Tesla was blocking whose." Abigail laughed. She shook a finger playfully at Willow. "Don't go making trouble for me now."

Willow felt a chill roll down her spine, an ice cube sliding over her skin.

Suddenly, a chorus of buzzes and rings cut through the air.

Abigail looked at her phone. "Shit."

A sweaty man in a suit burst through the kitchen door. "We just got an alert. The fire. They're evacuating the hills."

Willow's heart seized. Sunny, Aso. They were back at the van.

Willow ran to the kitchen door. As she pushed it open, she looked back. Abigail's eyes were wide.

Willow shoved her way through the bustle of guests. Her throat was constricting, but she closed her eyes, kept going. There was no time for a panic attack now. She had to get to Sunny.

She burst out of the house. The smoke clawed at her lungs. A burnt-orange sky hung low, as though night had fallen and a hellish sun had risen in its place.

Willow kicked off her heels, left them lying in the grass. The rocky earth scraped at the bare soles of her feet as she rushed down a staircase tucked between the houses. The streetlights had gone out. She hoped she was going the right way to the Rose Garden. She held her hands out in front of her, praying she wouldn't bump into anything. She'd left her green dress behind.

As she turned the corner, she saw someone pounding on the door of a house, yelling, "Anybody home? We have to evacuate!"

She wondered if anyone had knocked on the van's door, to check if they had gotten out.

Then she saw them. Sunny standing with Aso, scratching him behind his ears. Willow sprinted, her eyes blurring with tears. She collided into Sunny's arms, almost throwing him to the ground.

"Whoa, whoa, hey, babe," Sunny said, smiling and pulling away to look at her. "You okay? What happened to the party? We just stepped out, heard some commotion."

"The fire is coming," Willow said breathlessly, brushing away tears, drawing streaks of ashy wetness down her cheeks. She crouched to hug Aso, inhaling his doggy smell.

"There's an alert to evacuate," she said. "We have to go."

They climbed into the van, and Willow told Sunny in a rush of words what happened at the party. How it was full of so many people, so many greasy fingers, so many crumpled napkins. How they'd crowded around her, saying horrible things. How she'd smiled and held her tongue. And how she'd seen the blaze coming, tried to warn Abigail that it was too close. How Abigail hadn't listened.

"Babe, I'm so sorry," Sunny said, moving to wrap his arms around her.

"No, Sunny, there's no time," Willow said, pulling away. She didn't know why, but the last thing she wanted was to be held. Her mind reeled back to that night, all those years ago. The way she'd felt trapped, suffocated. Her mouth filled with an acidity she couldn't swallow.

What she really wanted was to disappear. To be a wisp of air, to float away from it all.

Flames were shooting up at the end of the street, climbing up houses like a lit match. Willow felt a panic creep up her throat.

Sunny turned the key and the van sputtered, then fell silent.

"No, no, no, not now." He turned the key again—a gurgle and then a dying out. "Fuck!" He banged the steering wheel. "Okay. We're out of gas. We have to run."

Willow jumped as an ember exploded with a loud pop and a shower of sparks on the windshield.

Sunny opened the back doors of the van and Aso leapt out. As Willow crawled toward the doorway, she saw the dog run down a stairway between two houses.

"Aso!" they both yelled.

Willow clambered out and ran after the dog. She staggered as a wall of flames barreled downhill, its heat swaying her momentarily backward.

Her skin prickled. The smoke was so thick she couldn't see her hands stretched out in front of her. A series of crashes in the distance. Trees felled, cars crushed, windows smashed.

She couldn't tell which direction Aso had gone.

Her flesh singed. But she was used to pain. She even sought it out at times. Thought she deserved it.

A flicker of a thought, unwanted but still there, in that familiar voice that spoke to her only in the dark of night: *Maybe this was meant to be.* This meeting with the flames. Maybe this was what she'd been waiting for all along. A last surge of pain, and then the promise of nothing. Emptiness. A long respite.

No more mornings having to gather strength. No more rooms full of strangers, unexpectedly crowded.

A sweet peace.

Her body was writhing now. She wrapped her arms around herself, uselessly. She couldn't take this much longer, the sizzling ache of her skin. The air grew louder, the whoosh of the descending flames enveloped her.

Her eyes burned, and she shut them tight. She was at home in the dark.

She thought: *Mama. I won't make trouble for you now.*

The crackle and growl of the blaze drowned out Sunny's voice behind her, screaming her name.

———

Xavier saw his moms absorbed in conversation in a corner of the party, and he took the chance to sneak out. He ran the couple of blocks from Marcia's back to their house, passing through the kitchen and grabbing beers from the fridge, calculating that his moms might notice that they were gone later, but it would be worth it. He stopped by the bathroom to check himself in the mirror, pulling up his Jimi Hendrix T-shirt and flexing his abs. Whatever.

His moms called him their "beautiful boy," his bubbe "my handsome boychik." But there was only one person whose opinion mattered, and she would be over any minute.

The doorbell rang, and Xavier slid across the hardwood floor to the entrance. He paused to give a last glance in the hallway mirror, pulling vaguely at the ends of his curls before opening the door.

"Hey," he said, trying to sound relaxed, hearing the awkward break in his voice.

Mar's hair was tucked behind her ears. A narrow strip of skin was visible between her tank top and the high waist of her jeans. He'd never seen anyone so beautiful.

"Hey," she said back. She seemed nervous, and it comforted Xavier to know he wasn't the only one.

They went up to his room and he put on his carefully curated "max chill" playlist. Mar sat on the edge of his bed, flipping through his sketches. Her legs were crossed, a single bare foot tapping along to the music, "'03 Bonnie & Clyde." Xavier decided that he liked every single thing about her. The way she bit her lip when she was concentrating. The scar on her left shoulder, which she got from falling out of a hammock while camping as a kid.

Xavier was a squirrel, inching along a long branch. There was a high chance that it could snap at any moment, sending him careening through the air, splattering on the ground below. But he'd also seen squirrels make unimaginable leaps. They scurried and jumped into the abyss between trees, their long furry bodies hanging in midair for an impossibly tense second, their soft underbellies exposed, before they landed on the tip of another branch and rushed up toward the trunk, home free.

He looked at Mar. "You hear about that study on how most people don't think in actual words?"

She cocked her head to one side. His stomach lit up with desire.

"So apparently, not everybody thinks in full sentences in their head," he went on, swallowing hard. "Most people actually barely have an internal monologue at all."

Mar scrunched her eyebrows skeptically. "I feel like I'm always having elaborate conversations with myself. Aren't you?"

Xavier hesitated. With Mar, when he tried to give his usual responses—cocky, nonchalant—it landed flat. Shockingly, the more himself he was, the more bumbling and awkward and sincere, the more she seemed to warm to him, like she was peeling back the layers of his fake personas, and finding the raw, unsure boy in the center, and she actually liked him.

"Honestly I kind of wish I didn't think so much," Xavier said, watching Mar's face for a sign of confusion, anything that might toss him back across the gulf to being alone, misunderstood. "Like maybe if I didn't debate stuff so much in my head before I said it, I'd feel more . . . real."

Mar paused, and he felt his stomach plummet. He'd said too much.

"Yeah, I feel that," Mar said. Xavier breathed again. "So, what are you thinking right now?"

"Um, right this second?"

"Yeah, right this second."

He looked at her. "That this is nice," he said slowly. "That I like being here with you."

He saw her lower lip curl inward, her front teeth pressing into her flesh as she considered him. He took a breath. Then, like a squirrel, all soft underbelly exposed, he leaned in.

His lips were on hers, full and soft. She exhaled and he could feel the warmth of her breath playing through the hairs of his underdeveloped mustache. He started to laugh.

"What?" Mar said, pulling away and wiping her mouth self-consciously.

"No, nothing," he said, reaching for her hand and threading his fingers through hers. The thought occurred to him—already laced with the ache of nostalgia—that life would probably never get any better than this right here. "You're just . . . everything."

———

Looking at Xavier, seeing the tentative curve of his smile, his eyelids half-closed, heavy with longing, Mar wondered how she'd kept herself from letting him in for so long. She knew she'd had her reasons—how a crush could be distracting, and love painful. Lena's words played in her head: loosen up, live a little. Letting go felt so much better than keeping it together.

Mar traced a finger along the ridge of Xavier's cheekbone, then over the curve of his nose, the arch of his brow. The features she'd grown to know so well became new under her touch. She curved her hand behind his head, tugged gently at the curls at the base of his neck. His head snapped back willingly and sent a rush of warmth through her.

"Come here," she said, leaning back onto his bed.

Xavier's breath trembled as he leaned over her, pressing his hips against hers. She liked feeling his weight on her, being gently smothered. She reached up and tenderly pulled his glasses from his face, folding them and setting them on the nightstand. She peeled his T-shirt over his head. When he lay on top of her, she felt his heart beating wildly against her breast.

"Can I?" he asked, slipping a hand tentatively up her tank top and resting it on her belly, waiting.

She nodded, watching how he looked at her as he pulled her shirt off. He paused, swallowing hard, taking in the newness of her breasts, partly exposed. She felt powerful as he drank her in.

Then, with an almost imperceptible pew, like a critter emitting a tiny scream, the lights went out.

"What the hell?" Xavier said, leaning up on his forearms and gazing around the dark room.

Mar took a moment to admire the curve of his bicep through the glow coming in the window. How it drew a smooth arch from the crook of his elbow to the hollow of his armpit. One day, she thought, she would bury her face in him, inhale his smell fully. But it was still early for such abandon.

She followed his gaze to the window. The sky was dark. Not the bluish black of early evening, but a charcoal gray run through with red.

Mar looked at her phone. No service. She could hear shouts in the distance. Then a loud pop, and another.

"Fuck, we gotta go."

Mar rushed over to join Xavier at the window. Tall flames were approaching the other end of the house. She felt her breath catch in her throat. The blare of an alarm rang through the air.

Mar ran to grab her bag. She froze momentarily. Her parents didn't know where she was.

Xavier went to the other side of the room and unclasped the glass case above his desk, pulling out feathers and unpinning the small paper tags underneath each one.

"X, what the hell are you doing? Let's go!" Mar opened the

bedroom door and a rush of smoke came hurtling in, sending her tumbling back. She kicked the door shut. "Not that way."

She turned and Xavier was still collecting feathers. "Xavier, hello!"

"Yes! Sorry, um . . ." He glanced at the window. "The pool! If we climb out that window, it's not that far of a jump to the water."

"Okay," Mar said apprehensively. She tugged the window open, waving away the smoke that rushed in. She sat on the edge of the window frame, her legs dangling. It looked pretty damn high to her. She turned around. She couldn't see Xavier through the fumes.

"X, I'm jumping, okay?" she yelled, feeling the heat scalding her skin.

"I'm right behind you." He coughed. "Go!"

The flames moved over from the doorway, crackling up the wall below her. She closed her eyes and jumped.

The water received her. She floated to the bottom of the pool, and for a moment, she stayed there, finding a relief in the silence, in her weightlessness. Then she kicked, spluttering and coughing as she burst through the surface. She swam to the edge and crawled out.

Xavier's mother was standing there, looking at the house, her eyes wide with panic.

"Where is he?" Taylor asked, helping Mar to stand. "And where's your shirt?"

Mar looked down and felt a wave of horror as she realized she'd forgotten to put her tank top back on. "Um, we were just—"

"It doesn't matter." Taylor looked back up at the window. "Is that him? Why is he still up there?"

Mar followed Taylor's gaze to the window. A vague silhouette was visible through the smoke. A gust of wind blew flames farther up the wall, pushing them back from the heat. As the whoosh of the blaze grew to a roar, Taylor screamed. The raw, guttural sound cut through the air. Even in the intense heat, Mar felt a chill run down her spine.

PART III

fire

OCTOBER

The fire had stopped where they always said it would—on Shattuck Avenue, where the wide four-lane thoroughfare left enough berth for the flames to lick across but not catch, enough space for a dozen fire trucks to line up and form a wall. The firefighters, exhausted and drenched in sweat under their full-body gear, sprayed into the unforgiving blaze. After days of battling sky-high flames that leapt monstrously from treetops to rooftops and back again, the incarcerated firefighters began to wonder if it was worth it for the meager pay, the single dollar per hour, the short escape from the confines of a six-by-eight-foot cell, to be suffocated like this, to hover so close to death. It was under their persistent efforts that the flames were finally calmed, reduced to a smolder, then contained. The houses behind their line of defense, whose insurance was priced lower for just this reason, were spared. But the fifteen-by-ten-block stretch from Marin to La Loma Avenues, once a maze of towering Victorians, lush citrus trees, and worn-out swing sets, had become a field of ash.

The sheer speed of the fire's descent caught officials by

surprise, how it barreled down the two-mile stretch of hill in less than an hour. Climate change, they said, shaking their heads, a gesture that absolved many and satisfied few.

Sitting in the hospital waiting room, Taylor's heart was racing from the last twelve hours. Even inside the sterile space, she could still smell a faint odor of burnt, like something had rotted on the inside of her nostrils, lingered there, a reminder of what they'd survived.

She kept replaying the moment she realized Xavier was still inside the house, behind a wall of flames, beyond her reach. It was a torture unlike anything she'd ever experienced—the knowledge that her boy was suffering and, mere feet away, she couldn't get to him.

Then, like a twisted angel fallen from the sky, his body came hurtling through the flames, landing with a splash in the pool.

As Xavier swam gasping to the edge, Abigail came running down from the other house. As soon as she saw him, Abigail burst into tears—quite unhelpfully, Taylor thought. Mar, still soaking wet in her bra, helped Taylor to shoulder Xavier, limping and coughing, to the back of the car, where he vomited and then lay still. They drove downhill through narrow, one-way streets. With the power out, the only light came from the blaze at their backs. The cars moved at an infernally slow pace, trapped in a long line of neighbors trying to evacuate, honking desperately and uselessly at one another. Mar held Xavier's head in her lap, stroking his hair. Taylor glanced in the rearview mirror, felt a twinge of envy that those weren't her fingers tracing comfort across her son's brow. At one point, a man with threadbare clothes and a wild look in his eyes came running down, banging on the windows of the cars behind them. When no one let him in, he continued his race away from the flames. Taylor felt a wave of relief that he hadn't tried to get into their car. She didn't know if she would have opened the doors. As they inched toward the hospital, she prayed silently, suddenly quite religious in her desperation: *Lord, if you let us survive this, I will do anything. I'll never doubt you again, I'll be grateful for my life every day, I won't leave Abigail, just please let us make it through this night.*

"Family of Xavier Hayes-Foer?" a nurse called from the doorway.

"Yes!" Taylor and Abigail sat up in unison.

The nurse, clad in turquoise scrubs that absurdly reminded Taylor of spearmint gum, walked over and sat across from them. "Your son is going to be just fine," she said gently.

Abigail let out a loud sob and clapped her hand over her mouth. Taylor felt irrationally annoyed. She nodded at the nurse to keep going.

The woman explained that Xavier had second-degree burns on his forearms and clouding in his lungs from the smoke, but it should all heal over the next few days, weeks at most. They were still running tests to ensure there wasn't any long-term damage from all the ash that he inhaled. Meanwhile, they'd put him on a light sedative and some pain meds.

"He is awake now and asking for his moms."

They followed the nurse through the doors and down a long, blindingly bright hallway. Taylor frowned as she caught her reflection in a mirror: Who was that woman with the crazy eyes, in an oversize Oakland Medical Center T-shirt? She flashed back to a couple of hours earlier, when she waited with Mar outside the hospital doors for her parents. The girl was shivering, shirtless. Taylor took off her blouse and handed it to her. When she went back inside—after a flurry of thanks and confused glances at her bra from Mar's parents—Taylor walked straight into the hospital gift shop and bought a T-shirt, a bottle of water, and some Advil.

When they got to Xavier's room, Taylor exhaled in relief. Their son was sitting up in bed, his arms wrapped in bandages, a tired smile on his lips. "Thank you," she said to God, under her breath.

Taylor walked over to Xavier and ran a hand across his forehead. She gently rubbed his scalp with her fingers, like he used to ask her to when he was a little boy: "Mama, scratch my head."

Xavier looked up at her. "Where's Mar? Is she okay?"

"She's fine, honey. Her parents came to get her. You rest. Everything is going to be okay."

Xavier fell back asleep, his telltale snore filling the room. Taylor felt Abigail staring at her, but she didn't lift her eyes to look.

If it weren't for that stupid party. She couldn't help but think: Had she been eating chocolate mousse cake while the flames crept toward their house? Had she been laughing politely at someone's bad joke, sipping champagne as the smoke filled her son's bedroom?

"Should we get some food?" Abigail finally said.

Taylor hesitated. The last thing she wanted was to lose sight of Xavier again, but her wife was right. She was starving.

As they stood in line for pizza in the hospital cafeteria, Abigail opened her mouth and then shut it again. Twice.

"What is it, Abby?" Taylor said impatiently.

"You know what I keep thinking? It's ridiculous, but—Xavier's college applications," Abigail said. "That art project he's been working on for months for RISD, the one with all the feathers and the recordings? What if it all went up in smoke?"

"Jesus Christ, Abigail," Taylor said, mustering every ounce of self-control to not just walk away.

"I know, I said it was ridiculous. I just can't think about our house being turned into ash, okay? I need something—anything—to focus on, other than that. Our whole lives just . . . gone."

Taylor felt a lightness blossom in her chest. She stifled a smile, knowing how absurd it would look. Their entire life—gone.

She could start over. Make a clean break. She could go somewhere else entirely, leave the Bay, where she'd been born and raised, had grown up and grown old, could see the rest of her years unfolding before her like a high-speed train with no brakes.

She could live somewhere she could breathe, year-round.

Tears came to her eyes and fell in heavy drops down her cheeks and onto her chest.

"Oh, honey." Abigail wrapped her arms around her, surely thinking she was crying over the house.

Taylor felt the familiar press of her wife's hands on her back, the groove of Abigail's clavicle cupping her ear, a perfect pocket. What was she thinking? Of course she couldn't leave. What kind of monster abandoned her family at a time like this? And she'd promised God, after all. They'd been spared. She had to stay.

Taylor closed her eyes and leaned into Abigail, letting herself be held as she sobbed harder.

———

Some forty-five miles away, down Highway 880, beyond the wildlife refuge, eerily absent of birds that fled for clearer air, in the heart of San Jose, Gabriel sat in his old house—Camila's house—staring at the TV, unable to peel his eyes away from the news. The girls were curled up on the sofa, asleep.

After hours of frantic searching—first at Gabriel's apartment, then at emergency shelters—they had finally gotten a call from Mar. She was at the hospital. The cell towers had been down, so she wasn't able to call. She was with Xavier's moms. She was okay.

As Gabriel watched the figures on the broadcast mount—

thousands of houses burned, hundreds of people missing, dozens presumed dead—he wondered if his apartment was still standing. When they'd left his place after not finding Mar there, the flames had been barreling down the hill, practically on their heels. Now he regretted not grabbing more things while they were inside, like his guitar, a gift from his late father, or the shoebox of old photos of Mar as a baby. He'd fought so hard with Camila to keep those in the divorce—the mediator painstakingly asking which pictures should go to whom, who was in them versus who had taken them. Now his small victory rose like a bitter pill in his throat. If he hadn't insisted so hard that they were his, then they'd still be here at Camila's. Safe.

His stomach wrenched as he thought of his apartment. It had taken so long to get off the waitlist. The place had been wholly his in a way nowhere else really had in his life. It was not his parents' railroad house in Fresno, with the patchy lawn scattered with used car parts. Not his college dorm at UC Irvine, reeking of stale beer and strewn with his roommate's dirty laundry. Not this house, Camila's now, a one-story, two-bedroom bungalow that Camila had instantly fallen in love with, that they'd taken out exorbitant loans to pay for, that she'd filled to the brim with family photos and Oaxacan art. The apartment in Berkeley was the first time that Gabriel felt like he wasn't just someone's son, someone's teacher, someone's husband—maybe he was worth something as himself.

Yet now—looking at the way Mar's toes peeked out from under the sofa blanket and curled into Camila's thighs for warmth, how Camila's mouth hung half-open in that way it did when she dreamed, her upper lip pouting and swollen with slumber— Gabriel wondered if maybe he'd gotten it wrong.

With news of the firefighters searching the wreckage playing low in the background, the early afternoon sun pouring through the leaves of the ponytail plant he bought Camila for their tenth anniversary, he imagined for a moment that he'd never left. That he'd never fucked up and they'd never split. That he'd never moved out and Mar had never gone to that school and met that boy. That they'd never been invited to those people's party on the hill. Maybe this was the universe's way of telling him that this was where he belonged—right here, where he was Mar's father, could be Camila's husband again. He may have lost his apartment and everything he owned, but he could still be somebody to someone.

———

Back in Berkeley, inside an emergency shelter hastily set up in the CVS parking lot, Sunny felt like he was going crazy. He didn't understand how everyone was just sitting there on their cots, lined up against the wall, numbly staring into the distance. He'd drunk all the bottled water they'd handed out, eaten all the peanut butter crackers his roiling stomach would allow, which wasn't much. Every time someone walked through the tent flap, Sunny's head popped up, his heart clenched. But it was never her. Instead, a steady stream of the destitute padded in, those with nowhere else to go, who didn't have a car to escape in or friends nearby to crash with, who didn't have money for a hotel.

Sunny thought of all the people whose windows he'd knocked on, begging for a ride as he ran from the tower of flames at his back. Most stared straight ahead. Some waved him off. One even yelled, apparently livid at him for daring to ask. They all had somewhere to go, people to welcome them.

His skin crawling with angst, Sunny marched out of the Red Cross tent. If Willow was coming to the shelter, she would have arrived by now. He was going to go out and find her.

The air outside was hazy, reeking of dead things. Sunny climbed uphill, back to where the van had been parked. He didn't get far. A row of police cars blocked the road, an officer standing in the street with the unfortunate task of turning away people desperate to check on their homes.

As Sunny approached, he recognized the man. It was the same cop who woke them in the middle of the night, who forced Willow from their van in nothing but a T-shirt and underwear.

It dawned on Sunny that if it weren't for this guy making them leave their spot by the water, maybe they'd still be there. Maybe Aso would be fine, happily dozing in the back seat listening to the lapping waves. Maybe Willow wouldn't have had to run barefoot downhill to warn him. Maybe she would have gotten a ride away from that house. Maybe they'd all be together, safe.

Sunny felt the fury mounting in his chest as he walked up to the officer.

"Let me through," Sunny barked.

The officer took a step back, a look of tired resignation on his face, going through the motions.

"We can't let you in, sir," the cop said. He hadn't bothered with the "sir" when he was banging on the door of their van in the dark of night. "The area is dangerous. Many surfaces are still hot, and some of the items burning are likely releasing toxins. We need to clear it before we allow reentry."

Sunny looked past him up the hill. He took in the damage, which, with his tunnel vision on getting by, he somehow hadn't processed.

About a block up, the rows of houses, their fronts darkened

with ash, fell away completely. In their stead was a blanket of gray rubble, scattered with barely recognizable shapes—car frames, tree trunks, and chimneys, awkwardly standing alone. A light powder covered every surface. Sunny wondered how much of it was made up of burnt branches, how much charred homes, how much human flesh.

The anger went out of him all at once, replaced with a deep fatigue.

"Please," he said, locking eyes with the officer. "I just want to know if she's in there. If she's okay."

The cop shook his head slowly. "I'm sorry," he said, his first apology. No one was allowed in except emergency personnel.

Sunny turned away, then spun back around. "Do you know, if they found a dog while they were clearing things, where they would take him?"

The shelter on Shattuck, the cop said. Where Sunny had just come from.

"You know you can stay there, sir," the officer added. "If you need somewhere to sleep."

Sunny laughed, a harsh, bitter sound: "Oh, now you're worried about me having a safe place to sleep?"

He could still feel the violent glare of the officer's flashlight searing fear and shame into his bare chest at one a.m. The officer frowned in confusion, leaning in as though he'd misheard.

Sunny turned and left.

When he got back to the shelter, he lined up behind the others. He took a bottle of water and a pack of crackers. He sat on one of the dozens of cots against the wall.

A news banner scrolled across the TV: over one thousand homes had burned in the fire. He wondered if they included vans in the count. Probably not.

Sunny clicked open the locket hanging around his neck. The

tiny framed photo, held daintily between his dirt-encrusted fingernails, was spotless. Willow's mouth was open in a laugh. He
could hear it still, the tumble of her giggle, the way she sounded
out of breath at the end, gasping for air from how funny it all
was. His chest tightened and the image blurred as his eyes filled
with tears.

How come she hadn't run away from the flames? Where was
her instinct for self-preservation? He knew she was going after
Aso, but still, it didn't make sense.

He flashed back to the day, years ago, when he'd found her
lying in the back of the van, her head lolled to one side, vomit
trickling from the corner of her mouth, a dozen small white
pills in a pool of yellow-and-pink mess. Aso was barking and she
wasn't moving.

Sunny shook his head, forcing the image from his mind. He
looked back at the locket. Willow smiling, happy. Alive. He
closed his eyes, playing her laugh over and over in his head, willing it into being.

When she didn't show by sunset, Sunny dragged himself over
to the volunteers at the tent's entrance. He wrote down her
name (Willow Combley), her age (thirty-four), what she was
wearing (a white blouse and black slacks). He added her to the
list of the missing. She was number 239.

———

Abigail padded out onto the terrace and breathed in the clear
ocean air. The sun shone brightly. It felt almost like vacation.
Except it wasn't. They were here because a week ago, their home
had burned to the ground.

After calling a dozen hotels, they finally found one with a
vacancy that wasn't too far away: Les Palmes in Half Moon Bay,

about an hour's drive down the coast. When they arrived, the only room left amid the mass evacuations was an ocean-view suite. It was ridiculously expensive, but they were exhausted and desperate. And the insurance would cover it. The deck hung out over the beach below. It had a Jacuzzi in the bathroom. It was painfully beautiful.

For the first couple of days, Abigail had a piercing stomach-ache. It wasn't a symptom of menopause she recognized, so she decided it must be the guilt. It was unsettling waking up under a fluffy, starched white duvet each morning, knowing so many others were sleeping on couches or in their cars. But after a while, she got used to it (a person could get used to anything if you gave them long enough, luxury easiest of all). Eventually, Abigail began to think that maybe they deserved it. They'd survived a fire, after all, lost their home and everything they cherished over-night. They were allowed a semblance of peace.

She closed her eyes, delaying going back into the hotel room. She didn't want to face the rest of this impossible day, the first that officials were letting people back into the wreckage to see their properties and surveil the damage. Abigail held a hand to her throat, thinking of the house they'd lived in for fifteen years, reduced to soot.

She knew every nook and cranny of that house. The small, useless step up to the bathroom, which she snagged her foot on when she went to pee in the middle of the night, stubbing her toe, cursing silently and hopping on one foot in the dark. And the circle-shaped stain on the oak table. That table had cost a fortune, and Xavier casually left a bowl of cereal on it, overflowing with milk, seeping into the wood. What Abigail would give to have that table back, stain and all.

She took a deep breath and stepped inside. Taylor was getting dressed, huffing with frustration as she pulled a new, too-small sweater over her head. Xavier was sitting in a corner staring at his phone.

Abigail opened the closet. There were a handful of blouses hanging stiffly beside two beige sweaters that she'd hastily bought at Eileen Fisher. She missed her clothes. What did you wear to visit your home's ruins?

The three of them piled into the car and Taylor drove toward Berkeley, her fingers tapping nervously on the steering wheel. Xavier sat in the back, furiously typing into his phone, probably texting Mar, again. Abigail turned on the radio.

". . . fifty-eight confirmed fatalities, the second-highest death toll for a wildfire in state history," a somber voice said on NPR. "One has to wonder if this isn't the new normal for Calif—"

Taylor flicked it off.

As they climbed into the streets of their old neighborhood, the air shifted in the car. They stared out the windows.

It was unrecognizable. Block after block of what used to be houses were now yards filled with ash and melted black metal. The trees, which had only just turned from the deep green of summer to a soft yellow of fall, were bare, their spindly black branches reaching into the sky, a plea, unanswered. In the yards, Abigail identified a charred mailbox, a bed frame, a cast-iron pot, and a wheelbarrow with no handlebars. The undignified remains of a life.

Taylor slowed, struggling to locate the correct turns without the usual markers—the rainbow flag on the corner of Cragmont and Shasta was gone. So was the rosebush on Miller Avenue. Then they pulled up to a lot that they instantly recognized as theirs.

The house had disappeared, replaced by a rectangular pile of rubble. But Abigail knew this view by heart. The bright blue sky shined through the frame of their abandoned Subaru, landing like a slap.

Abigail reached over to grab Taylor's hand. Her wife's fingers closed tightly around hers.

This was it, then, Abigail thought. This was officially the worst day of her life.

She struggled to swallow. "How can it all just go away like this?"

She gathered the courage to open the door, stepping gingerly out into the gray field.

Taylor shook her head. "Can you imagine the people living in the houses still standing? Waking up each morning and looking out at this graveyard."

Abigail wondered what celestial randomness chose which houses to burn and which to spare.

Xavier handed them flour sifters they'd bought for the occasion. He'd seen them recommended in a Facebook group of survivors from a fire last year in Napa. They were good to sift the ash through, people said, to see if any small items were still salvageable amid the rubble.

He squatted down, dropping the sifter into the dust and tapping its side until the particles of ash fell through. All that remained were chunks of char. He dumped those out and moved on to the next square foot of decay.

Taylor and Abigail crouched down beside him. They dug through the remains of their home in silence. It occurred to Abigail that this was the first time they'd done anything together, all three of them, in . . . she didn't know how long.

As they sifted, Abigail found a few small, useless items: a rusted coin, a doorknob, a single earring. She struggled to hold them all in her palm as she continued to shake the sifter.

"You know," Taylor said, looking over after the third time Abigail dropped something and cursed, "if you just opened your hand up a bit, you could hold a lot more."

"If I let go, they'll fall out," Abigail said, gripping the items tightly in her palm.

"Just try, Abby. Open your hand." Taylor reached out to her, and Abigail pulled away.

"I'm fine!"

She got up, her knees and lower back screaming in pain. This was a waste of time. The things she cherished most had gone up in smoke: the old photos she had of her mother and father as young newlyweds; the scarf her grandmother had knit her "to keep warm in those horrid winters" at Smith, even though it was only a few degrees colder than New York; the love letters Taylor wrote her every year on her birthday. Come to think of it, she hadn't gotten one this year.

Abigail's phone vibrated. She pulled it out. REMINDER: BE GRATEFUL.

"Fuck off!" she screamed.

Taylor and Xavier froze. Abigail felt the tears running down her face before she even realized she was crying.

"We're going to rebuild, goddamn it," she said, her voice trembling. She wiped at her tears with the back of her wrist, her hands too filthy to do the job. They were going to get their house back, their lives back. They were going to spend time together. She and Taylor were going to be happy again.

"We're rebuilding this house, just as it was."

Xavier frowned. Taylor said nothing.

———

A mile away, down the ash-filled hillside, past the Rose Garden with no roses left to speak of, inside the tent of the emergency shelter, Sunny lay staring at the ceiling. He hadn't slept in days. Between the old woman on the cot to his left who played her handheld radio at all hours and his night terrors, with every thought of Willow gripping his organs, twisting them into knots, waking him from a fitful sleep, he couldn't find rest. There was still no sign of her.

Slowly but surely, the number of people in the shelter dwindled. Some found friends to stay with, others were placed in trailers by FEMA, others still were told their homes were standing, and they could go back now. But Sunny had nowhere to turn. The shelter was closing at the end of the week.

He'd gone by to see Jo at the community center, to ask whether they could get in touch with the landlord for the apartment he and Willow had applied for, see if he could move in a few days early. Jo shook their head, said they were so sorry. The apartment was no longer available. Apparently, the funds the organization was counting on fell through. The pledges the donors had made at that party—the one Willow had worked at—never materialized. The community center reached out to the attendees in the days after the fire. Some had lost their homes in the blaze. Others were choosing to redirect their philanthropic dollars toward rebuilding the hills. None, frankly, appeared very interested in revisiting a night that they'd barely gotten out of alive. Sunny and Willow's apartment would be going to someone else, a tenant who could pay full price. Likely another fire survivor, whose insurance could cover a year's rent up front.

It made sense to Sunny, the kind of sense that made him nod and laugh and also want to throw up. Of course it had turned out that way. It had always been too good to be true. That's not how things went for them. They got fucked, that's what happened. Every time.

Then, the cherry on top: his application for FEMA aid got rejected. He had no proof that he owned the van, let alone that it had been their home. The aid was meant for renters and home-owners.

So Sunny stared at the ceiling, unable to muster a reason to move, the vise grip tightening in his chest.

Through the crackling buzz of his neighbor's radio, a gruff voice said: "Unfortunately, as of this morning, any missing persons who have not yet been located should now be considered deceased."

The breath went out of him all at once.

A cry rang out, an ugly, wrenching sob. It was only after the old woman put her radio down, extended a handkerchief, that Sunny realized it had come from him.

He clutched the locket at his neck, his hand shaking and his breath coming in fast and shallow bursts. The old woman came to sit beside him, placed a hand on his back. He curled into her, wailing as she rubbed his shoulder. She rocked side to side, whispering something in a language he didn't recognize. Praying, maybe.

This was it, then. Willow, the love of his life, was gone.

His chest heaved, and his sobs morphed into a choked moan. He should have said something that night. He'd seen the smoke. Why didn't he realize that meant the fire was too close? Why didn't he stop her?

After what felt like hours, when all the snot and tears had poured out of him, his breath finally slowed to a wheeze, he took the old woman's hand and pressed it to his chest, a wordless thank-you. He left the tent, knowing instantly where he needed to go.

Bare plots of land stretched out before him as he climbed up-hill. The sign for the Rose Garden was still standing inexplicably amid the rubble. He walked over to the remains of their van, a shell of black steel propped up on four naked rims. The glass windows and everything inside had melted away.

He'd been coming to this spot for a few days now, leaving bowls of water and food on the ground in a far-fetched hope that Aso might still be out there, might get drawn back. Each morning, he came to check on the food and found it eaten. It was probably just some raccoon, a coyote, another woodland creature who'd had its habitat turned to dust.

Sunny dug through his pockets. He wanted something to bury in the last place Willow had been alive. His fingers climbed up to his chest, landing on the locket.

He crouched down at the foot of a tree—a tall, thin, black thing, an unwilling witness to the horror. He dug between its roots, his fingers stained with ash. He cast aside the gray soot until he made contact with soil. He removed the locket from his neck and pried it open. He brought the thin, sharp corner of the latch down into the center of his palm. He winced, digging into his flesh until a thin stream of blood trickled from his hand. He held his palm out over the hole, watching red drops turn black as they seeped into the earth.

"You and me against the world, baby," he whispered to the dirt.

Sunny clasped the locket back around his neck. He refilled the water bowl, poured out another pile of dog food that he'd gotten from the shelter. As he turned to leave, he heard a scuffle behind him. A small, filthy bear charged at him.

The beast shoved Sunny to the ground, smothered his face in drool. Sunny screamed in delight.

"Aso!"

The dog was covered in dirt and unidentifiable grime, jumping excitedly on his chest. Sunny laughed, furiously petting and hugging him. Aso's rib cage protruded newly from his sides. Sunny wiped the tears from his eyes, not caring that he was smearing blood and dirt down his face.

"I've missed you, boy," Sunny whispered.

He took his first full breath since the fire.

As soon as they walked into the food bank, the dog raced straight to the back. Sunny heard Jo's surprised squeal: "Fart monster!"

Their face dropped when they saw Sunny standing there alone.

"No sign of Willow?" they asked, stroking Aso despite his filth.

Sunny shook his head, unable to say the words out loud.

"Fuck," Jo said, their eyes filling with tears.

Sunny sat in the small office, staring numbly at the wall. He held on to the hot mug of tea and granola bar Jo handed him. He couldn't bring himself to eat it.

Jo told him how the lines of people waiting for food snaked all the way around the block now. How they would likely grow longer after the Red Cross pulled out. They offered to keep Aso while Sunny stayed at the shelter, knowing they didn't allow pets. But the thought of being separated from Aso again was too much. He would find another way. He just didn't know how quite yet.

"Hello?" A voice rang out from the entrance.

Sunny turned to see a woman carrying in a bulk pack of toilet paper and Cup Noodles.

"Hey, Abigail," Jo said. "Sunny, this is one of our volunteers."

Sunny nodded a greeting.

"I just came by to drop off some donations," the woman said. "How are you holding up, Jo?"

"Not great," Jo said, glancing at Sunny. "Do you remember Willow?"

"Of course," Abigail said. Sunny looked at her. "She was at my friend's house, actually, for an event, the night of the fire. I've been meaning to call her."

Sunny felt a hot fury in his chest. So this was *that* Abigail. The woman whose party Willow had worked at. The one whose friends hadn't kept up their commitments to fund the apartments. The one who hadn't listened when Willow warned her of the oncoming blaze.

"Willow's dead," Sunny said, spitting the words out, an accusation.

"I'm sorry, what?" Abigail's eyes darted from Jo to Sunny, her smile falling away. "How—"

"The fire," he said. He stood up and faced Abigail. She took a step back. "She told me what happened. How she tried to warn you about the flames being too close. How you didn't listen."

Abigail froze. "You know, that night . . . there was a lot going on. None of us knew, really, how bad it was. It surprised even the firefighters. The sheer speed of it. You have to know that."

Her eyes were a plea. She took him in, trailing from his furious glare down to his dirty T-shirt and his worn-out work boots.

A resolve settled in her face. "Where are you staying these days? Willow said you were living in a van."

"That's not your concern."

"I work in affordable housing," she said. "I can help."

Sunny shook his head. Nothing was available. Even the government people at the shelter were scrambling to find spots for those still there. Anyway, she was the last person he wanted help from.

"It's very difficult to find a place these days. Nearly impossible," Abigail went on, her eyes locking with Sunny's. "Unless you know the right people."

Some forty-five miles away, past Lake Merritt, where joggers flitted around the shoreline path, relishing the newly crisp, clear air; beyond the salt ponds of Eden Landing reserve, where the migrating surf scoters glided through the marsh, ducking their black heads and bright orange bills into the water in search of minnows; through the streets of San Jose, where the trees were still standing, full of leaves turning red and gold under the fall sun, Mar sat in the cafeteria of her old school, surrounded by her childhood friends, picking at her pizza, feeling more alone than ever.

When her mom said she'd be finishing out the school year back at San Jose High——avoiding a long commute to Berkeley, where she'd only spent a couple months anyhow and where her dad no longer went to work——Mar was relieved. She'd get to go back to the hallways she knew by heart, crack jokes with Rowan and Zoubida, bask in the comfort of not having to prove anything to anyone. So it was all the more unsettling when Zoubida recounted her night out with June——who'd invited her to the movies but didn't kiss her——and Mar had trouble focusing, stared off into the distance, felt totally uninterested.

Her friends had asked all the right questions——"Are you okay?" "What was it like?" "Can we do anything to help?"——but after Mar gave her answers——sort of, terrifying, not really——they'd moved on.

Mar pulled her phone out under the cafeteria table and typed: *Do you ever feel like laughing is a betrayal? Like, with everything that happened and people still suffering after the fire, it's not right or something?*

Immediately, three dots appeared. Xavier was good at that, being there when she needed him.

You're one of those people, you know, he wrote. *You lost your home. You had to change schools in the middle of the year. Worst of all, you live far away from me now*, he added with a wink emoji.

Mar stifled a laugh, not wanting her friends to notice her inattention. Only Xavier could get away with a joke like that.

What she didn't say, even to Xavier, was that she still felt like she was trapped in the fire sometimes. She smelled smoke and panicked, spinning around looking for the source, only to realize it was just a neighbor having a cookout. And if she stood for too long in the sun, the heat bearing down on her skin started to feel a lot like flames and she had to race over to the shade to calm down. She still had nightmares that Xavier was stuck in the house, up in his room, burning alive.

I keep thinking about the people who died, Xavier wrote. *Like, we lost our house, but my friend Alex . . . his grandma was too old to evacuate. She called his dad for help and they tried to get to her, but the roads were blocked with everyone trying to get out.*

Jesus.

Yeah.

Mar heard a snap and looked up to see Zoubida staring at her, her eyes wide with impatience: "Mar, hello? We've been talking to you?"

"Yes, sorry, I'm listening," Mar said, quickly typing: *sry gtg call you later.*

When she got home, Mar stepped into a familiar scene: her dad on the couch, watching the news. He had on the same T-shirt he'd been wearing when she left for school, and last night when she'd gone to bed.

"Hey, Papi," Mar said, tossing her backpack to the floor and leaning on the armrest beside him. "You eat anything today?"

Gabriel kept his eyes on the screen. Mar stared at the new, scruffy hairs extending out from his beard, chaotic and unruly.

"I'm gonna make myself some toast. You want toast?" she said, moving to the kitchen.

Mar had seen her mom try to summon him off the couch with her signature tough love—"Gordo, you can't just sit around all day. Did you apply for the renters' aid, like I told you? Anda, let's go."

Mar tried a different approach, a gentle coaxing. Neither seemed to do much. Gabriel had gotten it together just enough to call the school and request a leave of absence, but he hadn't done anything else since.

Mar brought over a piece of toast smothered in avocado with a sprinkle of cotija cheese and settled the plate in her dad's lap, tucking a napkin into his shirt.

"Gracias, mija," Gabriel said, reaching his hand up to squeeze hers, his eyes still locked on the screen. Back in the day, her dad's perpetual optimism and jokes used to annoy her. But now she'd give anything to hear his corny snort-laugh, instead of this selective mutism. Gabriel only broke his silence to curse at the TV.

"Hijos de . . ." Gabriel said under his breath as a news segment played about the county trying, and failing, to combat price-gouging after the fire. Rental costs skyrocketed throughout the Bay as demand rose from people who'd lost their homes and were looking to stay nearby until they could rebuild. And with so many homeowners being high-income earners with solid insurance, the market was flooded with cash, driving prices further up, entirely out of reach for everyone else.

Mar nudged the toast until her dad picked it up and took a bite.

She texted Xavier: *You know what it is? I'm not sad. I'm pissed.*
At who?
I don't know. The fire took out the whole hillside, right? Disasters

don't discriminate, rich or poor, everybody loses, blah blah. But you know what? Some people are going back to their old lives real quick. Meanwhile, others have had their whole existences wrecked. They'll never be the same.

Mar saw three dots appear. And then they went away.

She sighed and clicked over to Instagram. She read a post that Lena had forwarded her, from the "Berkeley Fire Survivors" group. It was by a Jo Toussaint. There was going to be a protest to mark one month since the fire. The theme was "Rebuild a Better Berkeley," planned by the local food bank. Organizers were calling for a radical redistribution of the land that burned. They wanted the city to cut back the size of private hillside plots to convert most of the land into affordable housing, to force any new projects by developers to commit at least half of permitted space to low-income rentals, to make all public land and parks open to tents for unhoused residents, and to ban sweeps and tows of any inhabited vehicles parked overnight.

"Let's turn this tragedy into a turning point," the post read. "Demand that Berkeley actually live up to its creed as a place that welcomes all people, not just the wealthy few."

Mar felt her heart race as she clicked through to Jo's profile and messaged: *How can I help?*

NOVEMBER

The breeze coming off the bay caressed Sunny's face as he dug his bare toes into the sand. He came here often, to the place where the city's cement foundations were swallowed by water. He came to remember Willow, how she used to step out of their van and walk to the bay's edge each morning, tilting her face up toward the sun, letting its warmth penetrate her skin and sear away the night's terrors. He heard a laugh behind him, and then a soft voice: "Me and you against the world, baby." He turned around. It couldn't be. Willow, in her green mermaid's dress. Alive. Sunny's breath caught in his throat and he ran, scooping her into his arms, pressing his face into the warmth of her skin, burying his nose into the crook of her neck, inhaling her. "What! How?" Sunny stammered incoherently, his face still pressed into her. He felt his chest grow warm where it met hers. The heat spread to his fingertips as he gripped her back. A sizzling sound bubbled through the air. His nostrils filled with the sharp smell of charred flesh. He stumbled back. Willow, swallowed by flames. "No!" Sunny screamed, lunging to push her into the sand, to stamp out the fire. He landed on the ground, his mouth filled with ash. "Willow!"

Sunny woke with a start, bathed in sweat. He sat up in bed, his heart beating wildly.

It took him a moment to get his bearings: a mattress against the wall, Aso at his feet, a small window with a tiny curtain blocking out the sun.

He exhaled and lay back, placing one hand on his chest and the other on his stomach, a trick Jo had taught him for when he felt a panic attack coming on. He closed his eyes and tried to slow his breath.

He was in a trailer that Abigail had secured for him. She'd worked her connections to get him a temporary RV from FEMA. Jo let him park behind the community center. Even though he'd been reluctant to accept Abigail's offer—the woman was clearly trying to rid herself of guilt, absolve herself of what happened to Willow—it was Aso that pushed Sunny over the edge. He needed somewhere safe to nurse the dog back to health. And figure out what the hell he was going to do next.

His boss from the construction company promised there would be work soon—a lot of it, in fact. Contracts were being signed left and right to rebuild the hills. But that was all still months away. The city had to clear debris and issue permits. Sunny's labor wasn't needed yet.

In the trailer, with nowhere to go, Sunny found it increasingly difficult to get out of bed each morning. He understood, in a way he never had before, all the times Willow couldn't rise from the sheets, a shapeless weight pressing down on her limbs. How the sun's enthusiasm hurt her eyes. Sunny had no appetite, food tasting sour in his mouth, turning to a dull paste as he reluctantly chewed the meals Jo dropped at his doorstep. On the worst days, he didn't answer their knocks, pulling the covers over his head to block out any sign of life. When he didn't respond, Jo would open the door and take Aso out, a generosity that Sunny didn't know how to repay.

Even on the good-enough days, when he sat in the parking lot tossing a ball for Aso, Sunny felt a thought pestering him, nudging through the tranquility: Wouldn't it be easier if he had just died in the fire? Then he wouldn't have to muster the energy to move from one impossible day to the next. He'd be with Willow, too, and they could feel nothing together.

At night, the terrors came crashing like waves. Each one started differently: he was in Los Angeles, back at his parents', or he was in San Francisco, sleeping under a pedestrian bridge. They all ended the same way: Willow appeared, he ran to her, held her for a brief, painfully tender moment, and then she burst into flames. He wondered if the trailer was haunted.

He couldn't explain it, but for some reason the RV felt smaller than their van used to, more claustrophobic. It was something about how the built-in furniture was distributed in the space, each item just inches away from the next. When he went to the bathroom, he bumped his head on the low doorway. As he sat on the toilet, his knees grazed the sink. The showerhead loomed above him, threatening to drench him if he turned the wrong knob. If he reached out an arm from bed, he could touch the edge of the kitchen counter. And when he coughed, the whole vehicle rocked underneath him, a boat without an anchor. If he managed to find some relief, some gratitude at having any shelter at all, a voice would prod him: Don't get too comfortable now. This isn't yours. It could all be taken away at any moment, will certainly be ripped out from under you soon enough.

Sunny sat up and pulled on a pair of sweatpants and a T-shirt——donations from the community center. He steeled himself for another day of painstaking rounds. First to the church on the corner, where he could get a hot breakfast, which more often than not he fed to Aso. Then to the food bank, where Jo would press him to take some groceries. Then to the corner of Shattuck and University, where he sat propped against the wall of the Mc-Donald's, a cup set out before him with a handwritten sign: LOST HOME IN FIRE. APPRECIATE ANYTHING YOU CAN SPARE.

In the first days after the blaze, he collected more than he'd expected. People went out of their way to cross the street, even putting their blinkers on and getting out of their cars, walking over with a look of deep concern in their eyes. "I'm so sorry," they said, bypassing the cup and stuffing a handful of bills directly into his hands. "Berkeley strong." But as the weeks passed, the people dwindled, the dollars diminished, and eventually those leaving McDonald's gripped their coffees in one hand, steaming bags of fries in the other, cast their eyes to the sidewalk, rushed past Sunny, avoiding his gaze.

At the community center, he found Jo sitting in the back office, head down, behind a giant stack of papers. The printer was squawking and buzzing as it churned out more files.

They wordlessly handed Aso a treat and Sunny a muffin, which he pushed to the side. He read one of the pamphlets they were printing out. Bold letters were stamped in all caps across the top of the page: REBUILD A BETTER BERKELEY. He wrinkled his nose and slowly read through the list of demands: redistribute land, build more affordable housing, ban homeless camp sweeps.

"So?" Jo said, their gaze loaded with expectation. "Coming to the protest?"

Sunny thought about the sign outside the church, which didn't say FOOD FOR THE HOMELESS but rather, FOOD FOR THOSE WHO LOST THEIR HOMES IN THE FIRE, a distinction that irked him.

He thought about all the clothing drives that had popped up in recent weeks, gathering coats and blankets for people whose belongings had burned. He knew he had the donors to thank for what little clothing and kitchenware he had. But where was all this charitable energy before the fire, when he and Willow spent frigid winter nights huddled with Aso in the back of their van, debating whether to turn on the car to get some heat or leave it off to save gas? He wanted to grab the people dropping off bags full of canned beans, smiling with self-satisfaction, wanted to shake them by the shoulders and yell: *Look at me! Am I worthy to you now? Is this what it takes? Now that some undiscriminating act of God took everything I had, am I allowed to need something?*

Sunny looked at Jo. "I'll be there."

———

A mile away, past Ohlone Dog Park, where a pit bull and an Aussiedoodle tussled in the dirt, up quaint Bonita Avenue, half-way between Vine and Rose Streets, inside a classic two-story, chestnut-shingled house, Xavier was deciding which sweatshirt to wear to the protest. He didn't have too many options. He'd rejected Mom Abby's appeals that he replenish his wardrobe with "college-appropriate" clothing (whatever that meant), opting instead for a handful of items from a thrift store—all black. He wanted his outsides to reflect his insides, dark and roiling as they were.

They had gone straight from the seaside hotel to a pictur-esque rental in North Berkeley. Seemingly overnight, the trap-pings of their lives had returned to an unsettling normalcy: back to school, back to homework, back to takeout from the ramen place on University Avenue. Xavier wanted to scream. His girl-friend was in San Jose, at a different school, her dad jobless and sleeping on her mom's couch. Others were lining up for food each morning at the church he passed on his way to school. And

Xavier was . . . fine. Except he wasn't, because when the sun poured into his room's window through the Japanese red maple, it looked like flames were dancing on the walls, and he broke out into a cold sweat, even vomiting once onto his new sneakers.

His moms kept asking how college applications were going; they were due in just a couple of weeks. But ever since Xavier had lost his feather collection in the fire, with all the audio samples he'd painstakingly collected, he couldn't muster the energy to start over. He didn't see the point. It all felt so far off, so fake, this idea of going to some school that was supposed to set him on a path to a picture-perfect life. He'd seen what happened to families with cookie-cutter lives: they burned to the ground.

What he really wanted was to get a piercing, or a tattoo—something to penetrate his body, to etch into his flesh the fact that he'd survived this thing that changed him. He would wait until school let out for the summer, when he'd be gone from this house, away from his moms' constant worried glances, finally on his own.

He slipped into a black hoodie with an anarchist *A* spray-painted on the back. As he walked into town, Xavier spotted a small nest tucked in the upper branches of an elm. He paused to listen to the peeps of hungry chicks, closing his eyes and inhaling, taking in the sounds of his most reliable companions. He'd read somewhere—late one night, when he couldn't sleep and unwisely Googled "what happens to birds in a wildfire"—that in the suffocating heat from the approaching flames, baby birds that couldn't yet fly launched themselves out of their nests in a desperate bid to escape. He imagined the small, featherless chicks landing in a splatter of broken wings and oozing intestines on the sidewalk. He played it over and over in his head, like a horrifying flipbook, the birds' panicked peeping, their clumsy hustle to the edge of the pile of sticks, so diligently and lovingly gathered by their parents, who hovered nearby, flapping wildly. And then the chicks' tumble through the air, the hollow crack of their tiny beaks against the cement. Then he *really* couldn't sleep. He considered texting the article to Mar—he shared everything with her—but then he thought maybe she didn't need the image of baby bird corpses keeping her up at night, too.

As he rounded the corner of Rose and Shattuck, he could hear the mounting fury of drums beating, a crackling megaphone, a chorus of calls and responses, bursts of cheers.

Dozens of people were gathered in the parking lot of the CVS, where the temporary emergency shelter closed days before. They marched in a circle, thrusting homemade signs into the air: BERKELEY FOR ALL, SHARE THE WEALTH, NUESTRA CASA ES TU CASA.

The crowd was growing as streams of people, a mix of old hippies, young families, and Cal students, poured in, some pausing to snap photos of themselves before melting into the throng.

Nervously scanning the crowd, Xavier spotted Mar. She wore an oversize black jacket he'd lent her—she liked wearing his things, because they smelled of him. Her crown of curls was pulled back with a bright red bandanna. She stood on the hood of a car, megaphone in hand, leading a chant: "What do we want? Housing! When do we want it? Now!" His stomach fluttered.

He looked up at the charred hillside, the blackened trees a reminder of what they'd lived through, an ominous warning of what was still to come. It felt right, this screaming, like something he could do: yell until his lungs gave out, demand something different, push for something more.

Xavier weaved through the crowd until he stood in Mar's line of sight. He caught her eye and she broke into a smile. She reached her hand out to him. When he got up on the car's roof, he saw the crowd had grown, likely numbered in the hundreds

now. Two old women held their fists in the air. A man with long
locks bounced a toddler on his shoulders, cupping his hands over
her ears to block out the noise. Someone with a shaved head and
a flowing rainbow skirt handed out pamphlets to newcomers.

A hawk soared overhead. Its wings outstretched, it drew
slow, ever-expanding circles in the sky, spiraling in celebration,
or in mourning.

Across the street, a small group of onlookers gathered. They
had come to take in the drama, but not participate. Xavier's gaze
landed on two women. They were standing side by side, their
arms crossed, mirroring each other's stance, facing away from
each other. His moms.

———

The bright sun was an affront to Gabriel, who had been perfectly
fine sitting on his sofa in the dark with the curtains drawn. But
Camila insisted, throwing him her warning glare, eyes wide,
nostrils flared, telling him that if he didn't come to the protest,
he would regret it. Ultimately, it was the fact that Mar helped to
organize the event and would be speaking that stirred some energy from deep within him, enabled him to move his lead-filled
legs, stuck as they'd been to the fabric of the couch.

As he stood in the streets of North Berkeley, across from the
bakery where he used to go in the mornings before school, Gabriel felt like a wholly different man. He used to greet the gap-
toothed Dominican barista each day with a joyous "Hermano!"
The old man would hand him his usual order of café con leche
with an equally bombastic "Profesor!" Now Gabriel felt "apa-
gado," as his mother used to call his father, after he drank too
many beers and sat in silence, the long day of backbreaking work
in the car repair shop fading into numbness. Turned off.

Gabriel glanced at the pamphlet Camila handed him.

"At least the kids get it," he said.

As he read through the protesters' demands, he thought about how he'd received a measly $1,500 from FEMA to cover his belongings lost in the blaze. With rental prices skyrocketing since the fire, he hadn't found anywhere to move remotely near the school.

"You do everything right, and just like that, poof, overnight, your whole life is gone," he said to Camila. "Y otra vez a empezar de cero. How can it work like this?"

"It's designed to work like this, gordo," Camila said, her eyes full of sympathy, or pity. He couldn't tell.

Gabriel listened to the protesters' chants: "Redistribute land! Give the people a fighting chance!"

Abigail and Taylor stood across the street. Abigail waved, and Gabriel gave a small wave back. He felt a familiar panic in his stomach. He wondered if they would tell the school they saw him here—one of the teachers, protesting. As progressive as the administration claimed to be, the principal did not welcome controversy. Even less so if it came from a member of the PTA. He was still on leave, but he hadn't lost hope that he would find his way out of this well of grief at some point, would ask for his job back. He stepped toward the edge of the crowd.

"Mr. Amado!"

Gabriel spun around to see Lena standing behind him, grinning, her silver hair gathered in a long braid down her back.

"You came to protest with us?" she said, her eyes wide in surprise. "Sick!"

She offered him a fist bump before melting into the crowd. Gabriel followed her silver hair as she darted over to a larger group of his twelfth graders. She climbed up onto the hood of a car. That's when Gabriel saw who she was standing next to, who all the kids were looking up to: Mar. She yelled, "Hey, hey! Ho, ho! Unfair housing has got to go!"

Gabriel felt tears come to his eyes. He nudged Camila and pointed at their daughter, her hair billowing around her like a sunflower. Camila nodded. "Our girl."

Gabriel's shoulders pulled back, he stood taller. He grabbed Camila's hand and dragged her into the mass of howlers. They came to stand below Mar. Her voice broke momentarily when she saw them. Then her yelling grew louder: "What do we want? Housing! When do we want it? Now!"

Taking a deep breath, Gabriel echoed his daughter's call, his eyes squinting against the sun, his throat raw. A wave of energy coursed through him unlike anything he'd felt since the fires, or long before. Camila frowned at him in mock surprise. He shrugged and reached for her hand, entwining his fingers in hers. She squeezed back. Then they turned to face Mar and roared.

———

Abigail didn't like seeing her son like that, on top of a car, yelling. He looked angry. Not like the respectful boy she'd raised. She supposed this was what kids did in their final year of high school. Stretched the boundaries of their independence, pushed up against the borders of their freedom. She just hoped the vehicle's owner wasn't anywhere nearby. From across the street, she caught Xavier's eye and waved. Her son looked away. She wrapped her scarf more tightly around her neck.

Abigail and Taylor had been on their way to buy Xavier's Hanukkah present—a bird feeder to place outside his window at the rental, to make it feel more like home—when they got drawn to the sound of drums beating and people shouting. When they came up on the rally, Abigail smiled. This was one of the things she loved about Berkeley: how you could count on people being fired up about one thing or another, young people and retirees joining together to express righteous outrage at the Chevron oil refinery pumping toxins into the air, or a new Whole Foods displacing a local Asian grocer. But her smile fell as she read the pamphlet a young woman thrust into her hand.

"What does 'rebuild the hills for the ninety-nine percent' even mean?" Abigail muttered to Taylor, careful to keep her voice low, in case other, perhaps more sympathetic, neighbors hovered nearby.

Taylor looked at the paper over Abigail's shoulder. "'Limit single-family plot sizes' . . . 'Allow for more low-income housing.' Makes sense," her wife said, in a tone Abigail recognized as combative but pretending to be reasonable.

"Well, obviously, I'm the first to say we need more affordable housing. Hello, my life's work," Abigail said. "I just don't know about making such extreme asks." She gestured at a line saying the city should buy out "excess land" from private lots to allocate to low-income, multi-unit homes. "There's a process for this kind of thing: community buy-in, permitting. There's a reason these systems exist, to make sure you're not overcrowding, for one, which could be a possible *fire* hazard."

Taylor snorted. "Well, that and the fact that their proposal would cut our lot down by about half."

"Well, yeah. Does that seem normal to you?"

Before Taylor could respond, Xavier walked over, holding hands with Mar. They had big smiles on their faces, a sheen of sweat on their foreheads despite the late autumn chill.

Xavier held out a clipboard with his free hand.

"Mom, Mama," Xavier said, more formally than Abigail would have liked. "Would you care to sign this petition to city council? Mar helped draft it."

"Hi, you two." Abigail read the petition, saw that it had the same demands the flyers did: shrink private hillside plots, give land over to low-income housing, ban sweeps of homeless camps.

Abigail hesitated, and then said: "You know, there really are some great ideas here. But I have to say, a few of these are a tad unrealistic, no? Like this one here." Abigail scanned the paper, then turned it to face Xavier and Mar, her finger digging into the page where it said, *Open parks up to tents for unhoused residents.*

"Our local parks are gathering spaces for families," Abigail went on. "Not exactly the kind of place you'd want full of people camping out, with all the hygiene and substance use issues that could entail."

"You know, families are unhoused, too," Mar said.

"Exactly," Xavier chimed in. "And a lot of people turn to substance use in the first place because they don't have safe housing. So if you're so worried about drugs—"

"Honey," Abigail cut in, a smile straining at the corners of her lips. "Don't you think the homeless deserve better accommodations than a bunch of tents in a park?"

"Well, obviously," Xavier said, growing agitated. "But they don't have that, do they? That's the whole point."

"Sweetheart, I'm afraid you're a bit out of your depth here. I've been working in affordable housing for more than half your life. I know you mean well, but you don't exactly know what you're talking about."

"So you're not going to sign it?" Xavier asked.

Mar chimed in: "It would make a huge difference to have the signature of someone so high up at a local nonprofit, you know."

Abigail could see the urgency in the kids' eyes. She looked back down at the paper.

"I'm sorry, I can't," she said, handing the clipboard back. "I just can't put the organization's name on something that I'm not sure I fully support."

Mar muttered: "Well, for someone who works in affordable housing, you'd really think . . ."

"You know what, Mar? You try for just one second to imagine not being a high schooler whose parents have taken care of everything for you, okay?" Abigail said. "And you try to work and build a life and make a home, to find some fucking purpose in this goddamn chaotic world, and then have it all vanish overnight, and then you come talk to me, okay?"

Abigail's breath was coming fast. She shook her head quickly, stepped back, suddenly embarrassed at her outburst.

"You know what, Mom?" Xavier said, his eyes narrowed in disgust. "Fuck you."

"Xavier!"

He marched off and Mar followed, turning to give Taylor and Abigail a small smile—apologetic or victorious? Abigail couldn't tell.

"Well, then," Abigail said. She turned to Taylor and scoffed in disbelief. Taylor was shaking her head—Abigail wasn't sure at whom.

Then, from behind her, Abigail heard a deep voice, dripping with sarcasm: "I should've known."

Abigail spun around to see Sunny standing there, unsettlingly close.

"Oh, hi, Sunny!" Abigail said, forcing herself to smile, taking a step back. She wondered how much of their conversation he'd overheard. "How's the trailer working out?"

Sunny smirked, his teeth bared. "Funny you mention it. I've been debating something for a while. And just now, you made this very easy."

He reached into the inside of his jacket, and Abigail felt her heart beating fast in her chest.

Sunny pulled his hand out and dropped a small, glistening object into the palm of her hand. A key.

"I'd rather not be indebted to someone who doesn't think people like me deserve to share public spaces with them."

"Sunny, that's not—"

But he had already turned away, swallowed by the teeming crowd, his pit bull trailing behind him. Abigail looked at Taylor, who was shaking her head again.

"What? What is it?" Abigail said. "Is there some way I've disappointed you, too? It seems to be the day for it."

Taylor looked up the street toward the charred hills of their old neighborhood. "Maybe it's good," she said, with a far-off look in her eyes, "that this all burned to the ground."

"How could you say that?"

"Xavier told me the other day how Indigenous communities used to set fires intentionally," Taylor said. "Prescribed burning, it's called. Clears away the dry, the decayed. Makes way for new growth."

"Our whole life turned to charcoal and you're waxing poetic about 'new growth'?" Abigail said, her voice trembling. "What exactly was it from our life that was so 'good' to have gone up in flames?"

"I almost died, you know," Taylor said quietly.

Abigail frowned. "Yes, we all almost died in the fire."

"No." Taylor locked eyes with Abigail, her gaze hardening. "Before. I was suffocating in our old life."

Now Abigail was the one who fell quiet.

Then after a pause: "I don't understand what you're saying."

"Of course you don't. Our life was always enough for you,"

Taylor said. "It was built around you. The money I made subsidized you quitting your corporate slog of a job to go into nonprofits. The time I spent raising Xavier——dragging him from school to soccer practice to piano to playdates——allowed you to spend all your time 'making a difference.' And what was left for me at the end of the day? You coming home exhausted? Our son complaining that I was 'hovering'? What exactly in our life was built for me? I'm allowed to want something, you know!" Taylor's volume rose with each sentence. "An inch, a fistful of happiness. Some fulfillment, something for myself!"

"Well, of course," Abigail said, her voice lowered, looking around, hoping Taylor would follow suit. "Why haven't you said any of this to me before?"

"When was I supposed to say it?!" Taylor was yelling now. "As you walked out the door in the morning, leaving me to clear up the mess of breakfast? On our one date night per quarter, when we actually had a moment to ourselves?"

"Okay, clearly we have a lot to discuss. At home. When we have some privacy."

"I'm telling you this now!" Taylor screamed, releasing a wild, throat-scratching cry.

She looked at Abigail, her lips curled. Then she turned and walked off.

Abigail stood still, staring at her wife's receding back. She smiled shakily, not daring to look around at who might have seen. She lifted a trembling hand to her throat.

PART IV

earth

APRIL

The soil was dark and damp with days of rain. The rare precipitation had soaked into the earth, moistening the tips of the fire-gnarled roots. Plants celebrated by shooting upward in fireworks of green tendrils and sprouts, so bright they almost pained the eye.

Gabriel sat in a circle of chairs, in the middle of a sparsely decorated room, listening to the patter of raindrops on the windows. Other people were speaking, but he hadn't yet found the courage, even after weeks of attending the sessions.

After the protests, something stirred in him. He didn't quite feel himself yet, but a small light had been turned on—dim, but there. He started taking walks in the mornings, circling the block, delighting in the tiny buds peeking through the neighbor's bushes. He trimmed his beard, finding new streaks of white and gray in it. But somehow, he was always spent by late afternoon. He'd get drawn back to the couch, end up staring at nothing.

Camila pressed him to try therapy. At first, Gabriel resisted, thinking of his father, who wouldn't divulge his feelings to a group of strangers if you held his sore, leathered feet to a flame.

But he wanted so badly to give Mar something different, to be something more for her than his father had been able to be for him.

So here he was, half listening, half praying no one would notice that he still hadn't said a word. A middle-aged woman, Maya, was talking about her son, who had addiction issues, and how she'd kicked him out of the house again, but still stayed up nights hoping he'd come back. And around the circle they went, some shaking their heads, others saying there was nothing she could do if her son didn't seek help for himself. The therapist asked how it was for her to know that she couldn't control her son's addiction, she could only control her response to it.

Gabriel snorted at that. How very Zen and unhelpful.

A dozen heads spun toward him, shocked that the new guy had expressed anything at all.

"Do you have a response you'd like to share?" the therapist asked gently.

Gabriel dug his fingers into his palms, trying to come up with an appropriate answer.

"I guess I just think it's easier said than done—accepting something so out of your control."

The therapist nodded. And slowly, reluctantly, Gabriel told them. How in one night, he'd gone from having his own place, building a life for himself after a grueling divorce, to suddenly being left with nothing—no space to himself, not a single object to his name, nothing to offer his daughter, just his own weight digging into his ex-wife's couch. He felt small and useless and couldn't escape the thought that it was pointless to try to start over. What for? It could all just burn down again.

"My wife—my ex—Camila, she tells me she's worried, leaving me alone when she goes to work. She thinks I might hurt myself."

"Will you?" the therapist asked.

Gabriel laughed. He stopped when no one else joined him.

"I don't know," he said, looking at his hands. "I know I don't want to be this person. So heavy. It's too much. For Camila. For Mar. But I also can't gather the energy to pretend I'm okay. Sometimes I wonder if maybe they'd be better off without me. Then they could move on, at least."

He kept his eyes trained on his hands. When no one else spoke, he looked up.

Maya had tears streaming down her face. The therapist nodded slowly.

"I used to think like that," said a young guy wearing an anime T-shirt. "I think maybe everybody does, at some point."

Gabriel inhaled, not realizing he'd been holding his breath.

"People can surprise you," Maya said. "You're over here thinking you're 'too heavy' for them. I bet they can handle more than you know."

Gabriel felt tears coming and he blinked them determinedly back.

"I can't speak for your ex or your daughter, but I know I'd be pretty upset if you weren't here next week," she said.

"Me too."

"Me too."

The therapist looked at Gabriel. "You matter to us."

Gabriel looked up at the ceiling.

"It's okay, man, you can cry here," anime T-shirt said. "You should have seen my sobbing ass last month."

They all laughed and Gabriel did, too. His tears fell and he did nothing to stop them.

———

The rain did its work, washing away the old, seeping deep into the earth, softening the hard crusts of ancient wounds, laying the conditions for new growth. Gabriel went on his morning walk, and Camila joined him. They strolled through the wetlands of the Alviso Marina, their footsteps pressing softly into the mud, leaving gentle traces. Gabriel pointed out birds whose names he'd learned from Mar: a snowy egret, not to be confused with a great egret (both big, both white, differing only in their relative size, the elegance of their stance, the colors of their bills). He told her about therapy, how they made him cry each week, but he said it laughing, so she knew they were good tears.

At home, Camila prepared breakfast. She took two eggs from the hot water earlier than the others, because he liked his yolk runny, like a river (she preferred hers firm, holding its own).

When she opened the dishwasher and found it full, she felt like crying. Some things were new and wonderful, and some things wrenched her straight back into the past. She lifted her head and already hated the sharpness in her voice when she asked Gabriel why he hadn't emptied the dishwasher like he said he would. He looked up from the paper and his gaze landed on her, his brow creasing, a plea or an admonition. He was quiet and she waited. She searched for the telltale signs, the glazing of his eyes, the slight pinching of his lips, the small ways he showed that he had shut down, that there was no more reaching him now. She anticipated how later he would tell her she was unfair, and also that he wasn't good enough, that she deserved better, that he was a worthless piece of shit.

But instead, he nodded. He said he was sorry, got up, came into the kitchen, began pulling lightly chipped coffee mugs from the machine. As he put the dishes in their rightful place, he told her she didn't need to raise her voice like that, though. He deserved better than that. And she was the one to go quiet, then.

She said he was right, that she was sorry, too. And she walked away slowly toward her room, unsure who this man was in her kitchen. Liking his firmness.

When she went to take a shower, saying she needed to cool down, she didn't close the door, on accident and on purpose. As she undressed, she could feel the heat of his gaze from the kitchen. She took off her jeans and pretended not to notice him watching. She unclasped her bra and let it fall to the floor and didn't rush to put it away. She kept her back to him, even though he'd seen her breasts countless times before—touched them, kissed them, sucked them the way she liked. And when she removed her underwear, she stood still longer than she otherwise might have. The water was running, a precious resource she didn't like to waste. But for a few seconds, she lingered. For a moment, she indulged in the tenderness of his enjoyment of her. And then she stepped into the shower, out of sight.

That night, after they watched TV, she rose from the couch and said she was going to bed. He reached for her hand and held it. His eyes asked: Should I come, too? And she was quiet and he waited, searching her face for something, anything.

She didn't move, only held his hand—not pulling him toward her, not pushing him away.

Because, how could she be sure? She had thought she'd known who he was so many times before, until he showed himself to be other. Thought him loyal to a fault, and then he strayed. Thought him principled, and then he caved. She could see how he'd grown, how he was working to change. And sometimes, she hated herself for being so hard on him. But was it really hard on him, or soft on herself, when she set a boundary and didn't let it come down? Because she didn't know, really, that he wouldn't go back to hating himself too much to let himself be loved, or to love her without needing her to take care of him. And the worst part, really, was that even now, just where he was, right where they were, she wasn't sure it was quite enough really.

She squeezed his hand and let it go. She went to her room and didn't ask him to follow. She slept in her bed (formerly theirs), and he slept on the couch. Because how could she be sure? How could one ever be sure of another?

———

The steady patter of raindrops against the roof mimicked the nervous flutter in Mar's chest. She lay still, counting down the minutes. She could feel the tendrils of her future unfurling somewhere just beyond her reach. In mere seconds, she would know. They both would. She and Xavier would open up their phones and tap on a page. They would see which seeds were planted, which futures dried up.

She needed this badly. Something to propel her out of this stuck place. The protests she'd worked so hard to organize fizzled out in a matter of days. Those who hadn't lost their homes lost interest—and perhaps liked how their property value soared. And those who had, didn't have time to keep taking to the streets day after day. They had listings to scour, aid to apply for, insurance companies to fight. The petition they filed with the city was mentioned briefly in a public hearing, set aside for later debate by the council, and ultimately tabled.

Back in San Jose, Mar's life took on an eerily familiar rhythm, as though everything were normal, except it wasn't. At school, she felt out of place, the low buzz of her anger unwelcome among her old friends, her sadness a bore. At home, her parents clung to each other in a confusing dance, her father still sleeping on the couch, but also doing her mom's laundry, watering her plants—things he didn't even do back when they were together. Her mom fed him mouthfuls of arroz con pollo as she cooked. But then she'd push him to apply for housing. He still spent nights staring at the news. Mar was sick of dangling between the before times and this muddled after. She wanted out.

She looked at the clock. Two minutes to go. As the rain fell, she stroked Xavier's bare back, scratching his scalp through his curls. He fiddled with the waistband of his boxers, which she was wearing. His eyes were wide open like hers, staring anxiously at nothing.

The alarm went off and a bolt of electricity shot through them. At first, neither of them moved. As badly as Mar wanted to check, she also wanted to linger awhile longer on this side of the knowing.

She sat up and pulled her phone out. Xavier put a shirt on. She gave him a small smile—okay, then. She clicked.

Tears came rushing to her eyes. All those hours studying, all those evenings turning her trauma inside out for college admissions, had paid off. She got into Brown.

She looked up at Xavier. His eyes were filled with tears, too.

"I got in," she said, smiling hesitantly.

He paused, looking at her. "Me too."

She lunged into his arms, her grin squeezing her eyes shut, stretching the sides of her cheeks.

She pulled back to look at him. "Hey," she said, pausing before the next part. "I love you."

Xavier froze. He peeled himself out from her grasp and stood up. "Um, I'm gonna head home and tell my moms the news, okay?"

"Okay . . ." Mar said, confused by his abruptness. She suddenly wished she hadn't said what she did. "You good?"

"Yeah, no, I'm great, I just . . . feel like my moms would want to know sooner than later." His hand was already on the door-knob. "I'll call you."

Mar watched Xavier leave. She shook her head quickly, determined not to let this get in the way of her joy. She didn't have time for a boy's stunted emotions right now. She knew someone who would want to dance around the room with her. Someone who loved her unabashedly.

Mar got dressed and stepped into the living room. Her mom and dad were on the sofa with books open in their laps, clearly waiting for her to come give them the news.

"Lo logré," she said.

"Órale!" Her dad jumped up and pulled her into a tight hug, squeezing the air right out of her lungs.

She laughed and looked over his shoulder at her mom. Camila was smiling calmly, like she knew all along that Mar would get in.

Gabriel stepped back and put his hands on Mar's shoulders, his face suddenly serious.

"You know we don't care what school you go to, right?" he said. "We're just happy if you're happy. You matter to us."

"I know, Papi," Mar said, rolling her eyes and waving away the intensity of his gaze.

As corny as her dad's earnestness felt, Mar was grateful to see some of his old self coming back. It would make it that much easier when the time came for her to leave them behind.

———

By the time Xavier got off the BART at North Berkeley, the rain had lightened to a thin mist. It hung coolly in the air, clinging to him. He'd spent the hour-long train ride with his head pressed against the window, staring dully at the houses of Fremont, the low-rises of Hayward, the skyscrapers of downtown Oakland, whipping by too fast for him to take in.

He couldn't believe he hadn't said anything to Mar. She'd said *I love you*, and he'd just left.

But he also knew he couldn't stay. He couldn't cope with the roller coaster of emotions rushing through him, didn't have the heart to tell her, seeing the excitement on her face, what really happened. He wanted her to celebrate her acceptance fully, unburdened by his disappointment.

He took out his phone and looked at the letter again. *We regret to inform you . . .*

The applicant pool was "particularly strong" this year, yada yada. The point was, he wasn't going to RISD. He wasn't going to sketch northeastern birds he'd never laid eyes on before: orange-breasted robins and bright red cardinals. He wasn't going to get out of figure-drawing class and stroll uphill to pick Mar up from bio, roaming the streets in search of the best boba in Providence.

Somehow, despite knowing how tough admissions were, how selective this school was, he'd taken for granted that he was going to get in. When Mom Abby said to him, over and over, when he was growing up, "You can be whoever you want to be," what he'd heard was that the world was his for the taking.

Xavier put his phone on silent, ignoring the eight missed calls from Mom and two texts from Mama. It dawned on him that this was the first time in his life that he'd failed at something.

When he got to the house, Xavier crouched low, moving away from the entrance and over to his bedroom window. He fiddled with the pane until it slid squeakily on its rails. (His moms would lose it if they knew how easy it was to break into this place.) He climbed in and grabbed a few items off his desk, some more out of the closet, and shoved them into a bag. Then he left.

When he got to Indian Rock Park, he marched up the massive boulder's carved-in steps until he reached the top. The mist had cleared and the wind howled ominously as it curved over the rock, threatening to knock him off balance. From up here, he could see all the way to the water.

If he looked past the bare, blackened trees dotting the hill and focused on the verdant bushes peppered through the flats, he could almost forget that the fire ever happened. The spring brought a maze of wisteria to the city's ledges, crowned its tree-tops with green buds and white apple blossoms.

One by one, he pulled the feathers from his bag. A black one laced with goldish-green hues—a Brewer's blackbird. Shorter, pale brown ones painted with a blue tint—mourning doves. A long gray one that tapered into a black tip flecked with white—belted kingfisher. He'd hastily collected them for his college application, attempting to re-create the audio-sensory bird box project he'd lost in the fire. Xavier pulled out a crow's blue-black plume, brought its softness up to his cheek. Then he tossed it into the wind. He watched as it curled and dipped, until it disappeared from view.

He knew then, watching the feathers he'd imprisoned twirl celebratorily in the wind, that he wasn't going to college.

He didn't want to be stuck in a classroom, seated in neat rows, molded into some tailored version of who he was supposed to become. He wanted to do something new, feel something other than the fury bubbling under the surface of his skin. He knew that, somehow, he had witnessed a crime—they all had, but no one cared. *Nothing to see here*, they all seemed to say. *This yearly sacrifice by fire? All normal, to be expected. Carry on.* But he couldn't.

He wasn't exactly sure what he would do instead, but he knew it had something to do with the trees he'd grown up surrounded by, the birds whose trills and hoots were the soundtrack to his loneliest moments, anchoring him. He wanted to give himself over to the earth.

As he walked home, Xavier thought about how, after a fire, black-backed and redheaded woodpeckers flourished, feasting on the fresh population of beetles and larvae that appeared suddenly, gnawing through the bare, blackened trunks. The critters finding treasure amid the char.

———

A mile away, past the adobe building of the Berkeley Public Library, whose rounded entryway invited wanderers down book-filled aisles; beyond the Edible Schoolyard, where middle schoolers dipped their fingers into the soil, pushed seedlings in, waited impatiently for tiny green shoots; inside a small front yard on Bonita Avenue, Abigail knelt in the garden, her knees propped on an old yoga mat in an attempt to ease her aching limbs. She pulled weeds impatiently out from beneath her rosebushes.

She'd planted them in the winter, and by some miracle (or by the grace of the rains), the plants had come up fully this spring, unfolding in velvet red and yellow petals with a powerful perfume. They were the one thing she could count on, her plants. The one thing that responded to her care.

Work had been painfully slow in recent months, as affordable housing projects were put on hold while construction crews were backlogged with all the rebuilding in the hills.

Ever since the protests, the atmosphere in the house had been taut. All three of them—Abigail, Taylor, and Xavier—felt as though they had said too much that day, and now said not enough.

Xavier spent his time outside school at Mar's. And Taylor seemed to perpetually be on her computer. So Abigail applied herself with an unusual fervor to her garden. Taylor noted more than once that it seemed silly to put such an effort into the yard of a rental they'd eventually be leaving. But Abigail was determined to make this place a home.

They'd tried, she and Taylor, after that mortifying public blowup. That night, they stayed up until dawn, with Taylor, suddenly a fountain of expression, bursting to explain her sense of suffocation, the intolerable smallness of her life. Abigail didn't know how to respond, failed to understand what exactly had changed, what she'd done wrong. "It's not you, it's us, it's all of it," Taylor said. "What more do you want?" Abigail pleaded. "You don't understand," Taylor accused.

They'd gone to a therapist that Marcia recommended, a short woman with frizzy hair who told them they had survived a "trauma" with the fire and had to "process" by expressing with "radical honesty" their deepest fears. Taylor: *This can't be it, everything burned, everything changed, and yet it's all still somehow just coffee and chores and dinner and repeat.* Abigail: *The world is on fire, and I can't help but wonder, is my life enough, is my work enough, am I enough?*

For a few days afterward, they settled into a new peace: they laughed more, even had sex—not the rote kind, where they rushed through a familiar sequence to climax, but slow and exploratory, lying lazily in bed afterward, caressing each other's skin. Taylor helped Abigail in the garden, and Abigail made Taylor her morning coffee. But then, gradually, like a barely visible fog descending around them, routine took hold—coffee, chores, dinner, repeat; is my life enough, is my work enough, am I enough. They found themselves back in their old positions, with a new knowledge of just how far apart they were: one the bastion of unhappiness, the other the guardian of hurt.

Abigail felt her pocket buzz, and she whipped off a dirt-encrusted glove, digging into her jeans. It was the contractor. They had just finished mounting the frame of the new house on their old property. He estimated that they'd be able to move back in by summer.

Tears sprang to her eyes. Maybe this was it. A way out of this nightmare. Something to look forward to.

As she rushed excitedly toward the house, her phone buzzed again. Glancing at the screen, Abigail hesitated before picking up on the last ring.

"Hi, Ma."

"So?" Naomi said. "Any news on the college front?"

"Oh," Abigail said, turning back toward her rosebushes, searching for any weeds she'd missed. "No, not yet. Xavier should be home soon, though. I'll let you know as soon as I do."

"The rabbi's son got into Dartmouth. Not too shabby."

Abigail felt a pinch and pulled her hand back from the bush. She sucked on her bloodied fingertip. Damn thorns.

"Good for the rabbi's son."

"Is Xavier not opening his admissions letters with you?" Naomi said. "That must be killing you."

Abigail rolled her eyes, annoyed, and also a bit surprised at how well her mother knew her. Then again, the problem was never that her mother didn't know her. It was that she did, and she didn't appear to like her very much.

"I did get some other news, Ma," Abigail said. "They've just completed rebuilding the outer walls of our house. We should be back home in a couple of months."

"Oh, that is wonderful, Abigail. Now you can put this whole dreadful situation behind you."

Well, it's not quite that easy, Abigail thought. But she wasn't going to argue. This was a good thing.

"You could come visit," she said, surprising herself. "Once we have the insides all finished, probably in the fall. We could drive up to Napa to see the foliage. Maybe do some apple picking."

"Oh, goodness, no." Naomi scoffed. "No, I learned my lesson the last time I was there. Best to stay in New York, where things don't suddenly go up in smoke!"

Abigail's eyes narrowed, her chest tightened. "You know what, Ma? That's it. I'm tapped out. My life was never good enough for you. Nothing I do ever measures up. And that's fine. But I'm done."

"Oh, come on now, Abby—" Naomi started.

But Abigail didn't hear the rest, because she hung up.

Her hands trembling, Abigail thought of calling her mother back to apologize. *Sorry for the outburst, Ma, the stresses of rebuilding and all that.* She looked over her garden, past the wood fence and into the tree-lined streets. Berkeley wasn't a city she'd grown up in, but over the years, it had grown on her. The sidewalks, cracked and uneven, felt so familiar that they were part of her now, ingrained in the wrinkles in her forehead, etched into the white hairs sprouting at her roots. She steadied herself. This was her life, goddamn it. She'd chosen it. And she was going to rebuild it, back to the way it was.

Stepping into the house, Abigail found Taylor making coffee at the kitchen island.

"Honey. The contractor just texted. The walls of our house are officially up!"

Taylor froze. She turned slowly around.

"That means we can move back in soon," Abigail tried again.

Taylor paused, then said: "Are you sure this is what you want?"

"Am I sure?" Abigail laughed at the absurdity. "A little late for that question now, isn't it? What else would you propose we do?"

"I don't know. We could sell! Move somewhere new. Start fresh," Taylor said, an excitement vibrating in her voice. "When

Xavier goes off to school, we could go somewhere we've never lived before, somewhere we can breathe year-round!"

Abigail shook her head quickly, a tension gripping her body. "But our whole lives are here. My work. Our friends . . . Xavier grew up here. We can't just— Where would we even—"

"I don't know!" Taylor said. "Paris. Mexico!"

"Mexico?" Abigail shook her head violently. "No, no, this is your fear talking. Remember what Dr. Rallen said, to watch out for when our fear talks. We can't just run away. There are still chores to do, dinners to prepare in Mexico, you know."

Abigail could see a flicker of light in Taylor's eyes snuffed out.

"I know you've been having a hard time," she tried again. "I just think I've found a way to do good here, you know? To contribute. Our city needs more affordable housing now than ever, after the fire. I just think we can build back our lives right here. Better than before. We don't have to run away."

"Do you ever wonder if maybe you're the one running away?" Taylor said coolly. "So determined to hold on to the life we had. What if what I'm asking for isn't running away? Can you fathom that this isn't the 'fear' talking, but *me* talking? What if I want a life that isn't made up of permits and galas? A life that we can't even imagine the contours of from where we're standing?"

Abigail could see her wife was trying to communicate her emotions, just like Dr. Rallen had instructed them to. But all she could feel was terror.

The front door banged shut and Xavier walked in.

His clothes were wet and he had an odd look in his eyes.

"So?" Abigail said, pasting a smile on.

He threw his backpack to the floor. He took a deep breath and said: "I'm not going to college."

"What!" Abigail and Taylor said in unison.

"I didn't get into RISD," Xavier said, almost defiantly.

"Oh, honey." Abigail moved to comfort him.

"No, it's fine," Xavier said, stepping back. "It was for a reason."

"Mishegoss. What reason?"

Xavier launched into a spiel about "not handing the powers that be your money for a degree you don't need" and not wanting to "participate in collective blindness to the climate crisis."

With every word from his mouth, Abigail felt her pulse quickening.

"Maybe I'll work for the forest service or something. I don't know. But I want to be useful," Xavier said, his eyes flitting from Abigail to Taylor, in search of some sign of approval. "After what happened last year, I can't just keep my head down while the world burns. I have to *do* something."

"Xavier, this is your future we're talking about," Abigail said, trying to keep her voice steady. "What are you supposed to do that's so useful without a degree? Earn peanuts and depend on government welfare?"

"Who said his options are college or welfare?" Taylor said.

Abigail whipped her gaze over to Taylor so fast she could have sworn something in her neck snapped.

"Life isn't a free-for-all, Taylor," she said, shaking. "There are structures and systems and ways to get to places. You don't just build a successful life out of wild dreams and thin air!"

"Stop!" Xavier yelled. "This is exactly what I don't want. I don't want you fighting over my future. I don't want you trying to scare me into going down some bullshit path. It's *my* future. I get to decide."

Abigail couldn't believe this. How did her son think they had paid for the privileged life he had up in the hills, with his birders' summer camps, his friggin' seltzer machine?

"Do you know how much less people without a college degree

earn over their lifetimes?" she said. "I know you're upset you didn't get in—"

"You don't know anything!" Xavier screamed. "You don't get it. I don't care about my income-earning potential. I don't want this life. I don't want to become you!"

Abigail felt the breath go out of her. She reached for a chair and sat down.

———

Taylor looked from Abigail to Xavier. She flashed back to the hazy day on the beach last fall when she'd pulled their son out of school, back before everything changed. She remembered how his eyes lit up when he spoke of wanting to build a birding app one day.

Part of her understood Abigail. She was terrified, too, of what might become of him if he didn't go to college, what options he was closing off for himself before he even got started.

But another part of her—one that had been growling beneath the surface in recent months, was all but screaming inside her now—knew full well what she'd gotten by doing everything right, by ticking off the milestones one by one, a checklist to fulfillment: it had all wound up wrong.

"Xavier, is this really what you want?" she said softly, locking eyes with him.

Xavier frowned, like he was unsure if this was a trick. "Yes," he said. "It is."

She could see the fear and uncertainty swirling behind the determination in his eyes. She desperately wanted to have all the answers for him. But she had none to give.

Maybe the pattern didn't have to repeat itself. Maybe he was onto something, in all his fervor, his youthful idealism—a way to leap into an existence that was free from all the "shoulds" that society dictated, a path to a life that was more true. Maybe they owed it to him to let him try.

"You're an adult now," Taylor said. "Just be prepared to live with the consequences."

"What the fuck?" Abigail stood up, staring in disbelief at Taylor.

The two women took each other in, seeing each other fully for the first time in months, perhaps years. Abigail, who gripped the back of her chair with trembling hands, clinging to the image of their house before the fire, the path she'd imagined for Xavier since he was a boy, to a relationship that had once bound her and Taylor so tightly it felt impossible that they could be standing this far apart now. And Taylor, whose body was rotated partway toward the door, her fingers spread open wide at her sides, stretching out her tension, reaching for what it might feel like to let go, to release the comforts that tied her down, to not just stay because she should.

Abigail pleaded: "Don't."

Taylor shook her head. "We don't have to do this anymore."

And she walked out.

As she climbed up to the den, she heard Abigail and Xavier arguing anew. Abigail would never forgive her for this. But Taylor also felt sure, deep in her bones, that the best way to love their son was to let him go—and that might be the best way to love herself, too.

She sat at her desk and ran her hand over the freshly waxed wood—a table bought hastily at West Elm, just like the rest of the furniture in this house, meant to fill rooms, to simulate a home after they'd lost theirs. But six months in, the sofa showed no worn, sunken places memorizing their shapes, and there were no notches in the wall where they'd measured Xavier's height as he grew. It was a home, but it wasn't theirs. And no amount of rebuilding, no fresh paint and newly laid floors, could bring that back.

———

The uneven ground poked at the bottom of the tent, through the sleeping bag and into Sunny's back. Everything was moist and cold, his clothes clinging damply to his body. Aso was curled up against him, trying to transmit his warmth. It smelled of rot despite Sunny's attempts to unzip the tent flaps occasionally and air it all out.

He rolled to one side and checked his phone: 6:52 a.m. One of the guys from the crew would be coming by any minute to pick him up on the way to the work site. Business was booming ever since the debris was cleared and permits were handed out to rebuild the hills. Sunny was working six days a week. It was grueling, especially on days like these, when the thin, cold rain came down in a shower of tiny drops, not heavy enough to call off construction, but humid enough to seep the spring chill into his goose-bumped flesh. But he couldn't afford to skip out on work for a single day. If he kept this up, his boss had promised to make him a full-timer by the end of the year. With that kind of money, he could save enough to get another van.

Sunny unzipped the tent and took a deep inhale, searching for a hint of breeze from the bay. He coughed, choking on the exhaust-filled air from the highway overhead. He'd chosen this spot because, if he stood on his tiptoes and looked west, he could just see the shoreline where he and Willow used to park along the water.

As his coworker drove them into the hills, the rain let up

and Sunny took in how much the hillside had changed in the six months since the fires, and how much had stayed the same.

The ground was a mottled gray now, properties cleared of debris but still wearing a coat of ash, a fossil imprint of the disaster. New spots of color sprouted up here and there: shocks of pale brown and beige, fresh wooden slats of new houses being built. Sunny thought people were crazy for rebuilding here. Hadn't they had enough? But he supposed he hadn't gone very far, either.

He sometimes wondered about why he stayed, now that Willow was gone. It was so tough to get by here. But nowhere else in the world made sense. He'd lived in the Bay for over a decade now. This was where he'd fallen in love, built his life. Where they'd adopted Aso. He knew when spring arrived by the smell of wisteria and citrus. The only other place he'd ever called home was Los Angeles, and he'd left that part of him behind long ago.

When they pulled up to the site, Sunny felt a shiver of recognition. The sign to the Rose Garden was up the block. They were near where the party had been. Where he'd lost Willow.

As they worked, Sunny tried to distract himself from the tension rising in his chest, the memories bursting forth: Screaming Willow's name into the dark, smoke-filled air. Running from the wall of heat, tumbling downhill, tears streaming filth down his face, into his mouth.

Sunny closed his eyes, practiced the lines Jo taught him: *Focus on what I can see, what I can feel.* He lifted a slab of wood and heaved it onto his shoulder, carrying it into what would eventually be the house's living room. He thought to himself: *I can feel this plank between my hands, I can smell its fresh wood, I can see the sky over this roofless shell of a house.*

He looked out at the view. The sun was coming out, and

the rain that had soaked into the soil billowed up in clouds of steam, giving the hillside a macabre glow.

He felt an anger churning inside him. Here he was, laboring to rebuild the hilltop mansions of the people who'd partied as the city burned. The ones who'd snapped photos at the protest only to lose interest days later. The ones who congratulated themselves for dropping off armfuls of donations at the center for the little people whose insurances didn't book them up in fancy hotels.

He knew they had lost their homes, too. They deserved to be able to rebuild, to move on. But he just couldn't shake the image from his mind: the owners of this house just a few months from now, stepping out onto their freshly sanded deck to look out at the view, admiring their new pool addition, the larger yard designed to create more defensible space against the next blaze.

And Sunny would not even be back to where he'd started. Worse. In a tent, sweating through the hot fall nights. The next time the smoke and fires came, they would close their double-paned windows, crank up their air purifiers, stay shielded indoors. And he'd be lying there, ash particles seeping through the tent's polyester lining, straight into his lungs. It was bullshit.

Sunny felt the urge to yell, to throw a wrench through the eight-by-ten-foot windowpanes lining the outer wall, watch the façade of this multimillion-dollar eyesore explode into a sea of glass.

He couldn't be here. Not now. Not when it was so close to where it all happened. Not when she wasn't here any longer. It was too much.

Sunny dropped his tools where he stood and walked out— he'd text an excuse to his boss later.

By the time he stepped into the community center, he didn't feel cold any longer. He was boiling, fuming with rage.

"Hey, you all right?" Jo said, rising from their chair.

The two kids who'd been hanging around the community center since the protests—Mar and Xavier—were there, sorting clothing donations by size and color.

Sunny paced the room, trying to get out the jumble of thoughts that had sent him running to Jo's door.

"It's all going back to the way it was," he said. "After everything that happened, the fire and all the charity drives and all the protests, is this it? It just goes back to how it was before?"

Jo shrugged.

Mar set the pile of sweaters she had in front of her to one side. "All these people will be back in their homes by the holidays," she echoed. "And then there's everyone else. The ones who lost more than a home—their livelihoods. Their stability. Their loved ones. Who can just barely muster the energy to get up from the couch."

Xavier picked at a loose thread on his sweater, pulling it until the string ran taut and then snapped. "And what's worse is the ones who think they're doing good in all this," he said, "who think they're making a difference, with their tax-deductible donations, their negotiations for barely affordable housing complexes, but actually they're part of the problem. They're complacent—complicit."

They stopped and looked at each other, unsure of where to go next. Sunny sloped down the wall, sitting on the floor. His breath came back slowly. Everything was still dark and heavy, but maybe he wasn't quite so alone.

———

Xavier rose as Sunny sat down. He began to pace the room, his footprints tracing Sunny's from one end of the office's squeaky floor to the other.

Sunny was right. This couldn't be it. Everyone just accepting all the lives wrecked and injustices laid bare. That this was just the way things were. He was youthful in his optimism, so full of righteous anger, not yet witness to enough disasters to have gotten worn down by all the ways the world could disappoint the hopeful.

"What if we made them pay?" Xavier said.

Sunny frowned.

"Who?" Jo asked.

"I don't know." Xavier was unsure of his motives or his aim. The direction of his anger felt very specific—almost painfully intimate—and vast all at once.

"The ones who moved on so fast they left the rest of us covered in their dust," Mar said.

Jo shook their head and Xavier couldn't tell if it was in disagreement or amusement.

Sunny broke his silence. "How would we do it?"

And then, like a flood released, or tinder ignited, all of them started speaking at once. They tossed thoughts around, some with tight jaws and an edge in their voices. They picked each idea up and popped it into their mouths, turned it over with their tongues, tasting its contours.

"We could protest," Mar tried.

"We already did that," said the others.

"We could write another letter to city council," Jo offered.

"You mean the same council that used our last petition to wipe their asses?"

"We could post on the center's Instagram page, call out the wealthy's hypocrisy."

"And what—lose the few high-net-worth donors we have?"

"Also, a million other accounts already do that shit—you see anything changing?"

Sunny mumbled something about what one of his cellmates said to him once in prison, years ago, about how you couldn't break down the system with its own tools.

"Audre Lorde," Jo said. "'The master's tools will never dismantle the master's house.'"

They all fell quiet. And then one of them spoke, and the air shifted.

An idea rolled into the middle of the room, an offering. The person who shared it did so almost jokingly at first, but then, when none of them laughed, they plowed on.

By evening's end, their eyes were glistening under the office's neon lights. Hungry.

———

The silence was eerie up in the hills in the dark of night. The few houses quickly built up were still shells of themselves, uninhabited. Streetlights that hadn't been wrecked by the fire glistened like tiny stars against a moonless sky. Two silhouettes approached a house on tiptoe, unnecessarily. Only the raccoons and owls were up at this hour. They got spooked a couple times, stepping on a wrench that clattered loudly against the cement, tripping over an abandoned plank left by the construction crew. The soles of their shoes pressed their imprints silently into the mud.

Their eyes adjusted to the dark, and they looked at each other only once, nodding to confirm they were still in this.

And then they went ahead, setting small piles of dried leaves and sticks about, nothing one wouldn't expect to find here any other day. Meant to appear natural. Accidental.

Then one by one, they lit them on fire.

It took a while for the flames to grow. The flickers climbed up and then receded. One of them, seeing the fire's struggle to catch, prayed silently that it might be snuffed out, that they might be given an alternative ending to this idea perhaps taken too far. But then, suddenly, like an answer, the blaze grew.

They stepped back from the golden light, from the emanating heat, as it climbed the thin, freshly built walls. One of them was brought reeling back to the night of horrors, their palms sweaty, their heart thumping loudly in their chest. The other was entangled in an altogether different fear: the off chance that someone might see their faces in the light of the flames, might recognize them. That they might get caught.

They comforted themselves with the feeling that this fire was surely different from the last, not coming down from above, but sparked from below, by their own hands. Not a random tragedy precipitated by human greed, but an intentional act, to send a message. A prescribed burn of sorts. To cleanse the old and rotten, make way for the new.

The residents of the flats, seeing the tall flames from their windows, sprang to action. Those who'd survived the last blaze panicked, struggling to breathe. They called the local firefighters, who threw on their gear, climbed into their trucks, prayed silently that this one wouldn't be as bad as the last. Within minutes, they drove up the hill, with no downward traffic obstructing them. Practiced hands by now, they stamped the fire out quickly. *Not this time, motherfucker.*

The ground, still a mud of humid ash and soil, saved them. The blaze didn't catch so easily without the hot, dry conditions ideal for spread. The fire stayed relatively contained, just a single tower of warning billowing up, and then snuffed out.

In the end, only one house burned.

The next day, the fire chief held a press conference in the parking lot outside CVS. She said they had the fast-acting citizens of this town to thank, not to mention the fast-moving firefighters—and the recent rains.

She gave her condolences to longtime residents and now two-time fire survivors Abigail Foer, Taylor Hayes, and their son, Xavier, whose new construction had turned to rubble.

Officials were still investigating, but so far they had gathered enough evidence to suspect arson.

They found two footprints embedded in the earth—sizes eight and ten.

———

Sunny didn't sleep for days. He stayed up, his mind racing in the dark, long hours of the night, waiting tensely for a flashlight to beam through the side of his tent, for the police to come and drag him away. He imagined them grilling him (it was always the same officer in his mind, with the goatee, from when he was seventeen, and, incongruously, his father, too, standing in a corner of the station, shaking his head). He told himself that he would never tell. He held on to the pact they'd made at the center, the four of them—Sunny, Jo, Xavier, and Mar: only they could ever know what really happened that night.

Speculation flew around town: posts on local message boards; whispers and guesswork that it must have been one of the protesters from after the last fires, angry that the city wasn't rebuilding the hills with the changes they'd demanded; rumors that it was the family itself, unhappy with the deal they'd gotten from their insurance, hoping to get more a second time around; and panic that it might not be the last house to burn, that the hills weren't safe to live in any longer.

———

Abigail couldn't focus at work, found it impossible to carry on a normal conversation at home. Her suspicions of who had ignited the fire gnawed at her insides, each one worse than the last. She kept quiet at dinner, her head spinning.

Could it have been Sunny, still angry at her for the loss of Willow on the night of her party, bitter that Abigail was getting to return home while he could never get his wife back?

Taylor picked idly at her sushi. Xavier texted, not even bothering to hide his phone under the table.

A thought tore through Abigail like a lightning bolt, cracking straight through her heart, seizing her chest until she couldn't breathe: Could it have been Xavier? Who'd yelled at her to fuck off, that he didn't want this life, didn't want to become her.

Her eyes flicked to her wife, who twirled a chunk of wasabi in soy sauce, stirring it with her chopstick long after all of the green had dissipated into the liquid.

Another thought, somehow worse, almost impossible to contemplate: maybe it was Taylor, who never wanted to rebuild in the first place, who said she'd been dying inside in the life they'd had before.

Once they had all gone to bed—Xavier to his room, Abigail to her own, Taylor to the den—Abigail waited. She watched the clock tick by until two a.m., an hour she was certain would find her loved ones fast asleep. Then she tiptoed over to her son's room, slipped in just to confirm what she already knew. As he snored lightly (a habit he'd developed in the last year, which somehow made him seem more of a man, more distant from her baby boy than ever), she lifted his sneakers, tossed carelessly in a corner. She flipped them over to look at the bottom: size ten.

She didn't have to check Taylor's shoes, knew her size from a lifetime of swapping footwear, putting on each other's sandals when their own pair was too far from the front door to bother retrieving: size eight.

Over the next few days—distracted, barely sleeping, head twisting with paranoia—Abigail decided on the only scenario that she could swallow, that didn't scald her throat going down: It was probably a stranger. One of the many people who'd been rallying against the housing complex she helped negotiate on the west side, for instance. Or, even better, maybe it wasn't a targeted attack at all; maybe it was random—stray vandalism gone wrong. An accident.

When the investigators came by the house to give them an update—they were still collecting samples from the soil, testing for any foreign objects that might provide some clues—Abigail stayed quiet, too afraid of the possible answers to ask questions. Taylor and Xavier said nothing.

As the cops stood to leave, Abigail blurted out a plea: "Stop looking." Their family just wanted to move on, she said. They weren't planning to press any charges.

One of the officers mumbled something about how it was "private property" so "technically" it was up to her, but they "didn't recommend letting a criminal get away with such an act."

The man, one hand on the radio on his belt and the other resting casually near his holster, turned to Taylor. Taylor's eyes flicked to Abigail, and that's when Abigail knew—the way you did with a lover whose face you'd memorized, whose expressions were part of your intimate vocabulary—she agreed. One of so few times they seemed to, lately.

Taylor stood and opened the front door, ushered the cops out.

What Abigail didn't say when Taylor came back in—as they locked eyes, with hesitant frowns carrying more questions than answers—was that she was terrified of what the cops might unearth if they kept digging.

———

If they had been dancing around each other before the arson, Taylor and Abigail were really putting on a show now: pirouettes around their suspicions, world-class frappés to avoid voicing these out loud, jetés to not wear through the fragile net that held them together. But Taylor was too tired to look at any of it too closely. She buried her speculations under the planks of the rental. Let them fester there.

Over the following days and weeks, the three of them resumed their fights of old, heightened by the inkling of betrayal in what had happened. Abigail pleaded with Xavier to not throw his life away by rejecting his college acceptances, and Xavier yelled at Abigail that she was a "tool of the man." Taylor hid in the den, turning to what had become an obsession of hers: visiting travel websites. She clicked through photos of far-off beaches, buried herself in reviews of coffee shops and open-air markets, checked the weather forecasts and air quality indexes in places miles and oceans away.

———

Xavier kept waiting for his moms to confront him about the fire. For them to ask if he knew anything about what happened that night. The longer it went on without them saying anything, the more of a joke it all felt to him—a thin veil of propriety doing a shit job of hiding the ocean of hurt and emptiness underneath.

———

Once the investigation officially closed, Mar breathed a sigh of relief. She could stop imagining her admission to Brown being snatched away, her future shriveling up just when it finally felt within reach.

She sat on the living room floor next to her dad, who was alphabetizing her mom's CD collection. He was on an organizing kick, something someone in his therapy group had said about the "feng shui of putting things away." Mar handed him another disc—Selena's *Amor Prohibido*—and thought that maybe the plan had been a bust. They'd had such high hopes: that they could wake people up, that things could be different from how they were before, that people could be shaken from their sleep, from carrying on with the old, that they could be pushed to not replicate the patterns that produced the fires in the first place. She didn't know whether they'd succeeded.

———

Over the following weeks and months, other houses went up in the hills. Only the burnt plot lay empty.

OCTOBER

Not far from city hall, where people folded away the tents they'd slept in the night before, triangulated between the Buddhist monastery, the brick synagogue, and the Baptist church, inside a trailer parked behind the community center, Sunny shook a sizzling pan from side to side, practicing flipping his eggs in midair.

"If you land another one of those on the floor, I'm calling the manager," Jo said, wincing in anticipation.

Sunny theatrically vibrated the pan, then with a flick of his wrist, sent the sunny-side-up egg flying. The jiggling yolk twisted dramatically in midair and then landed squarely in the center of Jo's plate.

"Now what do you have to say, huh?" Sunny said, grinning from ear to ear.

Jo laughed, and Sunny used his fork to pierce the yolk so it would drip down into the bed of rice. They sat at the small table folded out from the wall, tossing Aso fingerfuls of food as they ate.

In the year since the first fire—six months since the second—Sunny had found a steadiness he hadn't expected: he'd been able to find a trailer through a contact of Jo's, another fire survivor who'd moved back into their rebuilt house. The RV was a similar size to the one Abigail had secured for him all those months ago, but for whatever reason, it felt bigger. Maybe because it was his.

His boss had converted him to a full-timer, and, with the union's pay bump, he was making enough to buy the vehicle in monthly installments. Jo let him park it behind the food bank, which was convenient, since that's where he spent almost all his time outside of work anyhow.

In the mornings, Jo came over to have breakfast before the center opened. They occasionally brought over donated clothes that they knew he'd like: hooded sweatshirts with big pockets, work boots, size ten.

Over the past couple months, they had been planning a project together that had them giddy with excitement. So far, they'd pitched it to the usual donors. They'd received some nods, a lot of praise, a few donations, but not nearly enough. Jo said people were depleted after all the giving post-fire.

To really get the project off the ground, they needed one more critical piece—and Sunny knew just who to ask.

Later that morning, he stood outside the house. He hesitated before knocking, clearing his throat in an attempt to dislodge the knot of nerves gathered there. His mission felt fitting for a hot October day, on the anniversary of the blaze.

He reached for the ornate knocker before realizing it was just for show. He pushed a sleek white thing on the side of the door, poised under a camera lens. It sent off three sharp notes through the house. After a long pause, Sunny lifted his hand to ring again when the door opened.

Abigail shifted under the unfamiliar weight of her comforter, somehow rendered heavier with only her body lying beneath it. She stretched out slowly to relieve the pressure on her lower back—menopause, old age, who the hell knew. She stared dully up at the tiny spots of light dancing on the ceiling, thousands of little flecks reflected by the chandelier overhead.

She had been wrong, she realized, when they visited their house's ruins, when she thought she was living the worst day of her life. Actually, it might be this, right here. Waking up in their rented house, alone amid the vestiges of a life she'd grasped at but never fully held.

With Xavier and Taylor gone, Abigail hadn't had the strength to start rebuilding at the old property a second time around. It felt pointless. What was she going to do with so much space anyhow? She stayed at the place in the flats.

She took out her phone and scrolled through photos Taylor had posted on Facebook. The same woman appeared in several pictures, all voluminous hair, curvy waist, and tattoos running up her arms all the way to her neck. She couldn't be more different from Abigail. Or from Taylor. Her wife—her ex-wife, she supposed—had found the unconventional rebel she'd never dared to be herself.

In her more ungenerous moments, Abigail prayed for a hurricane to come down on the island and chase Taylor back to Berkeley.

She started to dial Taylor's number and then thought better of it. Instead, she called someone she hadn't spoken to in a long time.

"Abigail?"

"Hi, Ma."

She hadn't heard her mother's voice since she'd hung up on her last spring. She found herself getting choked up. She cleared her throat.

"I was just calling to check in, see how you were doing."

Her mother took an audible breath. "I'm glad you called, Abby. I've actually been meaning to speak with you."

There was an unfamiliar hesitancy in her mother's voice. Something close to trepidation. Or, perhaps, care.

"I've been talking to the rabbi," Naomi went on.

Abigail rolled her eyes, awaiting some advice to be imparted that she didn't ask for or need.

"About our last conversation. He suggested I might say some things to you. That could explain . . . how I can be sometimes."

"Okay." Abigail waited, dying to hear what her mother was going to say, and also terrified at the vulnerability in her mother's voice.

"I know I haven't always been fair to you," Naomi said. "I just always had this sense that you thought my life small."

Abigail closed her eyes. Her heart tightened. "I never thought that, Ma."

"No, I know, I know. Just give me a second here," Naomi said. "Ever since you were a girl, you were always off somewhere, doing God knows what. Spending the summer in some village in Central America. Moving cross-country the second you graduated. Leaving a perfectly decent corporate job to earn peanuts working for the homeless.

"Your life just didn't look like what I'd pictured for you, is all," her mother said, rushing through her words like she was barreling through a storm. "You know me. I met your father on the same block in Brooklyn Heights he and I grew up on. And I never left. You just frighten me sometimes, Abigail."

Abigail felt tears well up. This was about as close to *I'm proud of you* as she would ever get from her mother.

"I hear you, Ma," Abigail said. "Thank you for saying that."

"All right. Okay, good. Well, I should go," Naomi said. "I have to get ready for shabbos."

Abigail smiled. It was still hours from sundown on the East Coast. She'd never known a person to run faster from an emotion than her mother.

"I'll book a flight," Naomi added quickly. "We can go pick those apples in Napa you were talking about."

"That'd be nice, Ma," Abigail said. "I love you."

"Okay. Bye-bye, now."

Abigail chuckled. She hung up and pulled her eye mask from her hair, where it had gotten tangled in the night. Something to look forward to, she supposed.

She rose from bed and padded toward the kitchen. Her footsteps echoed against the hardwood. She'd have to get some more rugs.

Pouring hot water into the French press, she watched the grains swirl and gather at the bottom, rearranged.

When the doorbell rang, Abigail jumped. She glanced at her phone, peering at the fuzzy image from the outdoor camera. She frowned.

———

Sunny saw a panicked look fleet briefly across Abigail's face as she opened the door, before she broke into a smile.

"Sunny! How nice to see you." She gestured for him to come inside.

They'd been seeing a fair amount of each other lately. Over

the past couple of months, Abigail had been going to the center several times a week. And to Sunny's surprise, he had begun warming to the woman. There she was, day in, day out, handing out food, organizing donations, bringing in some of her own. He found it hard after a while to hold much against a person who kept showing up like that. After everything that happened, he could see some of her sharp edges softening a bit—or being worn down perhaps.

"What brings you all the way out here?" Abigail asked, moving to stand behind the kitchen island. "Can I offer you something to drink? Coffee? Tea? I've recently figured out how to use this espresso machine, and I make a mean cappuccino."

Sunny shook his head, slipping out of his work boots to avoid tracking dirt onto the clean floors.

"I actually have something to ask you." He sat on a stool, tucking his feet underneath him. "It's an idea we've been working on with Jo. We thought you might want to help."

Sunny delivered his pitch: they wanted to build a shelter for homeless youth.

It would be an extension of the community center. But the space would be more than just somewhere for young people to get food and rest. It would be a haven, welcoming teens who couldn't stay with family, but who didn't have anywhere else to turn.

"We'd call it Willow's House," Sunny said.

He paused, trying to read the frown on Abigail's face, her eyes flitting away from his.

"It would be a place for young people to feel safe. To help them figure out what's next," he said, determined to get through his pitch before she rejected it. "The thing is, we need more funding. As you know, that's tough to come by these days. Jo has been hitting up the center's usual donors, but we're short of what we need to get a large enough space to make this work."

Sunny told her that he and Jo had been in touch with Xavier and Mar. How Xavier had thought of an idea: for Abigail to organize another fundraiser, this time to benefit this new youth shelter. Put her networks to use for a good cause.

"We wouldn't have to raise all that much. Just a couple hundred thousand, to get the project started."

Sunny felt light-headed saying the figure out loud. What a difference having access to that kind of money would have made in his life. But he kept his voice steady, his poker face on. These weren't numbers that made someone like Abigail blink. He had to act like this was normal. A casual, totally doable thing. Which, for her, maybe it was.

"We'd only need enough for a preliminary rental, as we keep looking for something bigger, to buy outright. We want to get the project off the ground as soon as possible. When you're a teen with nowhere to go, every night in a warm bed counts."

———

Abigail was distracted. Her eyes kept being drawn to the pair of boots on the floor a few feet away. One of them, knocked sideways, had its sole facing her. She could read the bottom: size ten.

Her mind raced, back to the nights she'd stayed up contemplating all the people who might have burned their house down—again. She'd spent so long gnawing over the idea that it might have been Xavier, her own son, horrified at herself for even considering it. But now, the possibility that it was Sunny suddenly swallowed every other theory whole. It made sense. All the pieces added up.

She remembered when she started going to the community center more over the summer, after Taylor and Xavier left. Each time she crossed paths with Sunny, she would smile, but he barely acknowledged her. She wondered at the time if it was about what had happened to Willow. It did feel a bit much, after all that time, that he'd still be so upset—she wasn't even sure what for, frankly. She'd offered him a place to stay, at a time when nothing was available. He'd taken it, and then thrown it back in her face. She knew last winter was a stressful time for everyone, undoubtedly. And she also knew, from her work, that sometimes people who'd been living on the streets for a long time had trouble adjusting to being indoors again. She thought perhaps that was the real reason he'd rejected the trailer. But then, slowly but surely, Sunny's harshness fell away—he softened toward her, nodding hellos, sharing a table as they doled out food to the center's clients. These days, she even looked forward to seeing him. He and Jo were some of the people she talked to most.

But now, staring at the boots in her kitchen, the ground shifted under her feet all over again. If it was Sunny who'd burned her home, what did that mean? Was his softening born out of his guilt? If he'd set the fire, had he really meant to harm her?

"I thought you might want to help," Sunny was saying, his eyes trained on Abigail. "You know, Willow could have used a place like this, back when she was Xavier's age, off on her own."

Abigail shook her head, dizzy with her spinning thoughts. Then, from the recesses of her mind, a memory surfaced: She and Willow in the kitchen at Marcia's on the night of the party. Willow worrying about the smoke, the expanding glow. Her suggesting the partygoers leave, or at least move their cars. And Abigail waving her off, telling her to take the cake out, not to forget the candles.

She looked at Sunny.

Maybe it didn't matter. Maybe he had burned her house down. And maybe it was vengeance: a house for a soul.

Maybe this shelter was a chance to make things right. A shot at penance. For them both.

Or maybe he hadn't. And it wasn't.

The point was, this was a good thing, surely. Something she could contribute to. Something she could be part of. Something to make of herself.

———

Sunny couldn't tell what Abigail was thinking. She was frowning one second, her eyebrows arching the next. Her blinking sped up, and he didn't know if she was excited or appalled by his ask.

She came to sit on a stool beside him. "I don't know that I can host another fundraiser," she said. "Given the way the last one turned out. I think it might be a lot to ask the same people to raise money for yet another housing project. It could be triggering, you know."

Sunny felt his adrenaline come crashing down. Of course she wasn't going to help. He should have known. People never really changed, did they?

Abigail placed a hand on Sunny's arm. It took all of him to resist pulling away.

"I can do you one better, though," she said, a thrill blazing in her eyes.

She offered him the plot of her old house. The center could have the land to build the youth shelter on.

It was empty, because she hadn't known what to do with it without Taylor or Xavier around. She would donate it. All theirs, at no cost. A shelter with a view, right there, up on the hill.

"It would be a great use for our land," Abigail said, getting visibly emotional. "Something meaningful. We can figure out the logistics later."

Sunny shook his head. He couldn't believe it. He'd done it. He and Jo had done it. They would actually be able to make this happen. And what better place than the hills where Willow had last been alive?

"Thank you," Sunny said. He placed a hand over Abigail's and squeezed it. "Really."

He got up to leave before she could change her mind.

Abigail walked him to the door. "Thank *you*. For including me."

Sunny shrugged. "Whatever it takes."

He slid his boots back on, stepped through the house's front yard, a lightness coursing through him. A youth shelter was small in the grand scheme of things, he knew. But maybe it could change one person's life. Even many lives. He knew that if there'd been one around back when he needed it most, it certainly could have changed his.

The front gate yawned onto the street; rosebushes bloomed on either side. Sunny leaned over, buried his nose between the folds of a yellow flower, inhaled its sweet scent. He ran his fingers down its base and squeezed. A thorn embedded itself in his flesh. A drop of his blood fell into the soil.

Sunny brought his locket up to his lips and whispered: "It's you and me against . . ."

He paused, taking in the soft petals, how the stems twisted up in tall arcs from the earth, stretching toward the sun. "It's us making this world a bit better, baby."

———

Once Sunny left, Abigail danced through her house, floating on air. She imagined the shelter looking not unlike their old home, with a big open kitchen and a bunch of bedrooms, a deck where the young people could gather, take in the sun and the trees, a respite from the arduous roads they'd traveled. She could already hear young boys' laughter filling the space. She would drive there in the mornings, make pancakes, like she and Taylor used to for Xavier.

She wondered what her son was doing right at that moment. He was off somewhere, living out his anticapitalist fever dream. He committed boldly, bodily, to his convictions—something she wasn't sure she'd ever really done herself. She was proud, and terrified for him.

Maybe she would start a gardening club, get the young people into plants. Something to keep them out of trouble. She'd show them how to prune bonsai, to nurture easy-to-grow vegetables like carrots and herbs. They could cook together. She would make them feel loved, and she would be less alone.

She smiled, snorting as she thought of her mother. If this wasn't "making something of herself," she didn't know what was.

She thought for a moment of calling her mother back, to tell her. But then she knew exactly who to call. She dialed the number she knew by heart.

———

Three thousand miles away, past the dust-filled expanses of Death Valley, over the red cliffs of New Mexico, through the fast-rising wetlands of the Gulf Coast, beyond the disappearing islands of the Florida Keys, in a small town at the westernmost tip of Puerto Rico, Taylor woke from a nap to the unwelcome sound of her phone. It was a ringtone she reserved for one person only. She dreaded these calls, but answered every time.

Slipping out from underneath the sheets——a thin but necessary barrier against the rainy season's mosquitoes——she tiptoed out of the room, trying not to disturb the dozing body beside her.

"Hey," she said, just above a whisper, shutting the deck's door behind her.

"Hi," Abigail said.

"Was there something you needed?" Taylor asked, rubbing her still-sleepy eyes.

She looked out at the view. Bright green palm trees swayed in the afternoon breeze, rolling down the hill until they met a thin sliver of white sand caressing the turquoise coast. The ocean was different here, transparent as a bath, filling the air with a humidity that Taylor licked indulgently off her upper lip. In all her years in the Bay, she hadn't realized how she missed the pleasure of a warm night, or of a truly rainy day. The rain here came down in thick, confident drops——pouring in celebratory showers rather than hanging in the air, cold and thin. When it ran down her skin, Taylor felt like she was being cleansed in a holy water, awash in relief.

"Have you heard from our son?" Abigail asked.

She had taken to calling Xavier "our son" since Taylor left.

Taylor thought back to the tension running through their house last spring, after the arson. How when Xavier left, the last string that hung taut between her and Abigail snapped. And so, finally, she could go.

"He isn't taking my calls," Abigail said. "The last time we spoke, I suggested that he may have had enough of his little experiment and should come home, do something useful with his gap year."

"Has he been calling it a 'gap year,' Abby? Because if he isn't, maybe we should——"

"Our son is practically homeless, and you're debating semantics with me."

"He's not *homeless*," Taylor said, rolling her eyes, no one to see but the little yellow bird poised on the deck's railing—a reina mora, as Xavier helpfully identified when she sent him a picture.

Abigail fell silent for a moment, then said: "Sometimes I have nightmares, you know. That he's sleeping outdoors. And he's cold and shivering. And I can't get to him."

Taylor thought of her own night terrors: Xavier standing in the window, flames surrounding him, the heat pushing her back, keeping her from him. She woke up screaming.

"Abigail, you can't keep calling like this," Taylor said, in what she hoped wasn't too harsh a tone.

Last night, Gloria suggested that Taylor simply stop picking up. Taylor got defensive, protesting that they were in the middle of a divorce after over two decades together; they had a son, for God's sake; there were *things* they needed to talk about. Gloria just said: "It's called setting boundaries, amor," and walked away in that tranquil way of hers. Taylor thought that Abigail wouldn't know a boundary if it smacked her in the face. But clearly, she also had work to do in that department.

"You're right," Abigail said, her voice softening in a way that broke Taylor's heart. "You were right about a lot of things."

Taylor moved back into the house, away from the reggaeton playing next door. "Like what?"

"Like maybe I should have listened when you said you didn't want to rebuild," Abigail said. "Maybe it was a sign, what happened afterward, our house burning down—again. I think I was just afraid of what it would mean if we didn't build it back up, of losing more than we already had. And so I missed the cracks in it, maybe? Just how deep your unhappiness ran. And Xavier's."

Taylor was surprised at how she felt hearing those words,

which might have made a world of difference had they been spoken at a different time. She didn't find any satisfaction in being right.

A secret Taylor never spoke aloud was that she was grateful for the fire. The fires, plural. They had stripped her of everything she'd built out of a sense of obligation; taught her, in a brutal, violent way, how short life was. How precious. They'd forced her to live.

In the few months since she'd moved to the island, she'd begun working with a small women's clothing cooperative. They had a line of locally sourced leisure wear that they sold at farmers' markets and fairs. That's how she met Gloria, who she found standing behind a small booth on a hot day, her thick hair pulled back in a bun, sketching designs in her notebook. Taylor stopped, admiring the woman's intense focus as much as the dresses and overalls hanging about her, all soft cottons and linens in earthy shades of brown and dark green. When Taylor shyly told Gloria of her idea for a children's clothing line that expanded as kids grew, Gloria simply said: "Fenomenal. It appears that we were meant to meet."

"It's okay, Abby," Taylor said softly into the phone. "We all made mistakes." She meant it.

"I actually called because I'm doing something I think you might be interested in."

Taylor listened as Abigail told her about the youth shelter that the people from the community center wanted to build. How she'd offered up their old plot for it.

Taylor could hear the optimism in Abigail's voice. It had been a while since she'd heard anything but hurt and fear from her wife. It made her miss her.

"I thought this project could be a shot—our shot—to build something different here," Abigail said. "Like what you said before: something we couldn't even imagine the contours of from where we were standing."

Taylor let Abigail's words sink in. An invitation, an offering. To come back home.

She thought of how, as beautiful as Rincón was, sometimes at high noon, when eighty-six degrees of heat came pounding down from a radiant sun, she would do anything for a cool winter's day in Berkeley. For sweaters, warm socks, and hot coffee.

But then, a voice in her head: *You can't go back.*

She didn't want to be someone who was perpetually dissatisfied with where she was. For once in her life, she wanted to stay.

Abigail sighed into her silence. "You're not coming home, are you." A statement, not a question.

Taylor turned to see Gloria emerge from the bedroom, the smooth brown of her bare legs peeking out from underneath Taylor's button-down shirt. Taylor's gaze lingered on the flesh of her butt cheeks, the way they folded gently into the tops of her thighs, her backside vibrating lightly as she walked toward the kitchen in search of coffee. Taylor felt a pang of guilt at the happiness coursing through her. At how awake she felt. Taylor answered, gently but firmly: "I *am* home."

———

Deep in the valley, tucked between the tall pines of the Sierras and the sheer cliffs of Big Sur, some twenty miles from drought-shrunken Millerton Lake, triangulated between the Family Dollar, Dollar Tree, and Dollar General stores, inside a sweat-filled classroom in the heart of Fresno, Gabriel sat in a circle of his students and passed around a stack of papers.

He read the essay prompt aloud to his twelfth graders: "'If

you had a magic wand and could change one thing to make the world better, what would you do?'"

"Aw man, that's corny," Julio said, to a shower of snickers from his classmates.

"You know it! Aaand it's your assignment," Gabriel said, smiling. "You've got ten minutes to write out some notes, and then you're each going to share your genius ideas with the class."

After a few grumbles, the students picked up their pencils and started scribbling. Gabriel soaked in the quiet hum of a room of adolescents absorbed in their work, possibility buzzing in the air.

The classroom had become somewhat of a sanctuary for him, as he adjusted to living on his own. For a while last spring, he'd thought he might end up staying in San Jose. He was getting better, doing the therapy like Camila asked him to, slowly venturing outdoors, going for walks. But the intimacy he and Camila had felt from surviving the fires eventually waned, their familiarity souring with time. After so many months, his presence on her couch was clearly wearing on her, the couch's springs wearing on his back, and her not inviting him to their bed wearing on his soul. When Mar packed her bags for college, Gabriel packed his for the Central Valley.

He found a reasonably priced one-bedroom in Fresno, just blocks away from where he'd grown up. He got a job teaching at the local high school. And as he prepared for the new year, he made a promise to himself: it wouldn't be like before. All the things he'd gone through—the fire, losing his apartment, losing Camila (again)—it had to have been for something. He changed his curriculum, focused it less on the heroes of the past, more on the leaders of the present: community groups pushing for waste-water reuse; unions fighting for better conditions for outdoor workers laboring through heat waves. Instead of standing at the front of the classroom like he used to, Gabriel started each lesson by having his students pull their desks into a circle. He wanted them to know that he intended to learn as much from them as they from him, to understand that if there was a better future to carve out from inside this classroom, they'd have to figure it out together.

"All right, folks, pencils down. Who wants to share their idea with the class?"

A hand shot up, and Gabriel suppressed a smile. Kiara. She reminded him so much of Lena, full of big opinions and earnest fury. He nodded for her to speak.

"Okay, so, it's a tax fairy," Kiara said. Julio tsked skeptically.

"No, so listen. She's like the tooth fairy, but instead of leaving money for kids who lose their baby teeth, she takes money from giant corporations who don't pay their fair share of taxes."

Gabriel laughed, delighted.

"En serio, Mr. Amado," Kiara said, her eyebrows shooting up in mock indignation. "You know that if just, like, five major corporations paid the same proportion of taxes as the average American, we could eliminate all student debt in two years, or something?"

Gabriel nodded. "Fair enough." He wrote on the whiteboard: "Tax fairy—en serio."

The room rippled with giggles, and he turned back to face his students: "Who's got another one?"

That night, Gabriel sat at the small metal table in his kitchen and started his evening ritual. He didn't always send the letters he wrote. Some he tossed after reading them in the morning and finding them too trite. Others he kept in a stack, to perhaps send one day if he felt the urge. But occasionally, he mailed one off to Mar, writing to her because he didn't want to be calling all the time, but he wanted her to know he was there.

"I checked the weather for Providence and saw it's starting to drop into the forties at night," Gabriel wrote. "You tell me if that coat we got you isn't warm enough, okay, muñeca?"

What he really wanted to say was that she should be sure to soak up every minute on campus. That this might be the last time in her life when nothing more was asked of her than to simply learn, read for hours on end, absorb all the information she could get her hands on. She didn't know how precious that was. Before she knew it, all of that pent-up opportunity would come crashing into the brutal reality of life outside the college gates, and it would all feel far more mundane, more steeped in ordinariness than she would ever have imagined for herself.

But he couldn't write that. Those were the late-night musings of an old man, too heavy to burden her with, and not entirely true, either.

"It's funny, mija," he wrote instead. "When I was your age, I couldn't get out of this town fast enough. But you know what? I think I'm starting to see what your abuelos saw in this place."

That much was true. There was something about how, when he looked out the kitchen window, especially at dusk like this, he could see all the way up the street, beyond the stretch of one-story houses, past the burnt-orange, fall-crisped trees, all the way to the crop fields dyed gold by the setting sun. And it felt just for a moment like, if he were open to it, he could step into the wide-open expanse of the valley, grow tall as an artichoke stalk, and reach up toward the sky, blessed to be alive.

———

Over three thousand miles away, at the top of College Hill in Providence, Rhode Island, past the quaint cafes and gift shops lining Thayer Street, inside the concrete, seventies-style barricade that held the freshman dorms, Mar woke up in her narrow, extra-long bed, feeling like this place wasn't home.

She looked out the window, and the picturesque view was an affront to her loneliness.

A handful of lanky boys played hacky sack on a freshly cut lawn. Two girls in oversize sweaters leaned against a tree, poring over a massive textbook. Mar pressed her finger pads against the cold window, as though to absorb whatever energy they contained that allowed them to be so at ease here, to feel they belonged.

Ever since she arrived on campus, she'd felt like she was on the outside of a Christmas shop window looking in. Marveling at the toy train's colorful chugging, the porcelain doll's rosy cheeks and painted smile, a frame full of delightful things she couldn't bring herself to touch, not trusting the contours of their perfection.

When she felt lonely, she fantasized about leaving, hitchhiking cross-country, and meeting up with Xavier, wrapping herself in his arms, convincing herself that that would be enough.

The night she left for college, her things were stacked up all around her bedroom at her mom's place. Xavier sat on her bed, watching her put the last few items—a book, his hoodie—into her backpack for the flight. Her shoes, size eight, by the door.

Mar came to sit beside him and nuzzled her head into his neck. Nothing left to say. She traced a finger over Xavier's new tattoo, the ink still fresh, the skin on the underside of his bicep raw. TIKKUN OLAM, it said in Hebrew. *Repair the world.*

The thought of leaving him sent a flurry of panic into her stomach. The world beyond the Bay felt intimidating, a life without the security of his affection terrifyingly unmoored.

"Hey," Xavier said, placing a finger under her chin, lifting her gaze to meet his. "I love you."

"Hey," she said. "I love you, too. Maybe it's better this way. That we're ending things while we still love each other. Before we get a chance to grow sick of each other, or hurt each other too much."

Xavier nudged his glasses up his nose. She wrapped her arms around him, trying to memorize the way he felt—the warmth of his skin against hers, the press of her chest against his ribs, and her fingernails digging into his back, two puzzle pieces joined imperfectly, tenderly, together.

"Maybe this is just a break," Xavier said into her hair. "And in a few years, we'll meet again."

Mar tightened her grip, tucked her head farther into his chest, because she didn't want to let go, or because she didn't want him to see the doubt in her eyes. Or both.

Sitting on her dorm bed, Mar resisted the urge to send Xavier another text saying that she missed him.

She texted Lena instead: *You ever feel like you don't fit in at college? Like everybody else came here already knowing who they were, or how to be?*

Lena, miraculously awake given how early it was at UC Davis, texted back: *And here I was trying not to fit in with these dorks. I swear, if you come home over break wearing one of those puffer vests and horseback-riding-ass boots, I'm cutting you out.*

Mar laughed, responded with an emoji of a tongue sticking out.

She got dressed, debating whether to text Paloma—an intimidatingly cool girl she'd met at orientation—to ask if she wanted to walk to class together. She decided against it.

She curved through the twisted paths to the Lower Green, a carpet of gold leaves crunching beneath her feet, the air crisp with forewarning of a biting winter to come. She made her way to the sociology department, one of a half dozen quasi-identical brick buildings. After opening several wrong doors and backing apologetically out of them, she entered the lecture hall.

Paloma, seated in the front row, waved Mar over, removing her bag from the chair beside her. Mar blinked back tears of relief and hustled past other students to find her seat.

"Welcome," the professor said. "I'm pleased to see so many of you have decided to stay."

It was the day after "shopping period," when students who had been sampling different courses over the first few weeks of class decided which to commit to for the rest of the semester.

"As you all hopefully know by now, I'm Dr. Amarya Washington, and this class is 'Environmental Justice: Communities on the Front Lines of the Climate Crisis.'" Dr. Washington pulled a pair of thin-framed glasses from the pile of gray twists atop her head and rested them at the tip of her nose. "As I mentioned previously, this is not an introductory-level course. It is open only to juniors, seniors, and a handful of freshmen and sophomores in the climate justice program."

Dr. Washington gazed slowly around the room, the students poised at her every word. "Before we begin in earnest, I'd like each of you to introduce yourselves: please tell us your name, where you're from, and—most important—why you are here, in this class."

Mar felt her stomach clench. She knew why she was there. She was reminded of it every time the fire alarm went off in her dorm because someone forgot to open their window before lighting up, and she broke out in hives. She still hadn't told anyone about the fires. She didn't want to see their shocked faces morph into grimaces of pity, didn't want to hear "Well, at least you made it out, right? Objects can always be replaced."

Dr. Washington stared at her, and Mar realized it must be her turn. She shifted in her chair.

"Um, hi, I'm Mar Amado," she said, feeling her palms grow sweaty and sliding them under her thighs. "I'm from California." She glanced at Paloma, who nodded her encouragement.

"I'm in this class because I'm a climate disaster survivor."

A hush fell across the room. Paloma's hand came to rest lightly on her back. Mar leaned into it. "We lost our home in the Berkeley fires last year. And I want to study why, when everything burns, not everyone is left with scars."

Dr. Washington nodded slowly: "I'm glad you're here, Mar."

Mar latched onto the professor's words like a buoy in the open ocean.

After class, Mar and Paloma walked back toward the dorms. Paloma asked Mar about the fires. Mar hesitated, her eyes on the ground just ahead of her feet, trying to steady herself. She told Paloma how that night had started with a kiss that lit up her insides and ended with her plunged into darkness, jumping out a window, fleeing the unbearable heat of the flames. Paloma didn't gawk or pry. She told Mar how in Rincón, where she was from, they'd lived through Hurricane Maria. They hadn't lost their house, but her family had spent the night in a closet, the only room without windows, listening to the howling wind batter their roof, shatter all the glass, and cut the power. She told Mar about the wet, noise-filled darkness and how she still had nightmares about the roof caving in, burying her, smothering her screams.

Mar put a hand on Paloma's back, a thread unspooling between them, binding them to each other.

———

Somewhere deep in the woods of Northern California, past the rows of Santa Rosa houses that turned to ash years ago, beyond the town of Paradise, whose families were carried off in a plume of smoke, through the thousands of acres of torched firs, blackened pines, and scorched oaks in the graveyard of Mendocino National Forest, up hundreds of feet into the air, tucked in the branches of a redwood tree, Xavier sat on a rickety platform, wrapped in a sleeping bag, shivering against the cool night air.

As the sun set, its rays barely penetrating the pine-dense treetops, Xavier listened for the sounds of a spotted owl. He was here, in part, for that elusive bird, to protect it from the looming threat of deforestation. He was still bitter that he hadn't been able to record it last year for his audio project. But that all seemed so far away now. A different time. A different him.

Last spring, after the second fire wrecked their new house, settling its coat of suspicion onto his family, Xavier felt like he was suffocating under all the words left unsaid. As soon as school let out, he moved into Mar's mom's place in San Jose. Over the summer, he got involved with a group of young climate activists. Mom Abby would call, leaving long voice mails begging him to try one of the other schools he'd gotten into. Xavier deleted the messages. Come August, when Mar went off to school, Xavier hitched a ride with one of the guys. Noa, a lanky twenty-two-year-old with a wispy beard, was headed north, planning to join a protest deep in the woods outside Eureka, against a logging company that wanted to raze hundreds of acres of old-growth trees on ancestral Indigenous land. The moment Noa mentioned it, Xavier felt a wave of recognition wash over him: That's what he was going to do. What he was meant to do.

On the ride up, Noa pulled into a roadside thrift shop and suggested Xavier might want to trade in his all-black uniform for something more outdoor-friendly. Xavier bought secondhand flannel shirts, patch-riddled pants, and a pair of worn-out hiking boots, size ten. By the time they got to the campsite, Xavier looked like every other person there, gazing awestruck at the towering redwoods.

Dozens of tents were scattered around the forest floor. Ropes and pulleys dripped from branches, drawing Xavier's eye up to the wooden platforms nestled in the wide, ancient trees.

Around the firepit that first night, Bee Walker, one of the elders, welcomed the new arrivals. She introduced them to the forest they sat in, spoke of the trees, whose bases were so wide it took more than six people holding hands to wrap themselves around it. These trees had spent hundreds of years, some nearly two thousand, replenishing the air we all breathed, providing shelter, shade, and nourishment to the animals and plants, nurturing the herbs and fungi we ate, only to be unceremoniously chopped down by industrial loggers, carted off at such a rhythm that soon they would no longer exist. With the worsening fires in recent years, fueled by greed-laced emissions, the trees were disappearing at a previously unimaginable pace. Over the last two years alone, thousands of giant sequoias had burned, ridding the earth of nearly one-fifth of these precious giants.

"May we be stewards of this earth, our mother," Bee said, as the protesters reached around and held hands. "May we protect these ancient guardians from the profit-driven wreckage of capitalism. May we help stave off the worst of climate destruction for future generations."

As the others nodded, their eyes closed, Xavier took it all in, these people who he didn't know, whose radical mission he found himself suddenly bound to. Many were young like him, but others had faces lined with exhaustion, worn from years of fighting the same battles.

"Bless our enemies," Bee prayed. "Bless the loggers who will come in the morning. Bless those who don't see earth as our life source; help them understand that our fates are all tied to one another."

Xavier woke the next day to the sound of buzz saws ripping through the air, slicing into the early morning's peace. He stumbled through the woods toward the noise, finding at the end of the road leading to the camp five people seated in the middle of the wide asphalt lane, their arms linked. Two more had chained themselves to stumps, blocking the way. In front of them idled four massive trucks, their forty-foot-long beds empty, the drivers and other workers standing beside them, impatient. Some of the loggers were smoking indifferently, a couple honked their horns, others menacingly wielded their buzz saws in the air. But the protesters didn't move. Swaying side to side, they sang a slightly off-tune, haunting rendition of Marvin Gaye's "Mercy, Mercy Me."

Within the hour, a handful of cars from the sheriff's office rolled in. Officers got out and lazily delivered their warnings, well practiced in these inconveniences. They handcuffed the protesters' hands behind their backs and drove them off in their cars.

As the trucks moved into the forest, Noa placed an arm around Xavier's slumped shoulders.

"We'll bail them out, X. And then we'll do it again."

That night, Xavier volunteered to be one of the tree sitters. He wanted to know what it was like up in those tall branches, and if he was honest, he was nervous about befriending the other campers. He felt naive still, too much a child among a battle-worn clan. This way he'd be close to the birds, his stalwart companions.

Nestled up on his platform, his back leaning against the tree's knotted bark, Xavier listened to the sounds of evening falling on the forest: the buzz of insects and the twitter of chicka-dees and warblers hunting. Far below, he could just make out the area the loggers cleared that day: dozens of trunks were felled, scattered like so many matchsticks on the ground.

His phone vibrated in his shirt pocket. He pulled it out, sur-prised that he had service. One bar—probably captured by the sheer height of his perch. He read Mar's texts, smiling and feel-ing a sharp urge to cry. He sent back a photo of the sunset over the treetops, told her he'd look out for a spotted owl for her. Then he listened to a new voice mail from Mom.

She told him about her plan—to work with Sunny and Jo to build a youth shelter on the land of their old home. The rock-hard pit of anger Xavier had nurtured was chiseled down to a pebble. He heard the desperate hopefulness in her voice as she asked if he might come home to help build up the project. She understood he might not be ready to go to school just yet—said that was fine, really. She just thought this might be something that they could do together. Something like what he and Mar and the others had been demanding at the protests last year. A redistribution of land.

Alone among the birds and the trees, Xavier took a shaky breath, inhaling his uncertainty.

He couldn't go back just yet. He couldn't stomach sleeping in his old bed again, not when he knew that Noa and Bee and everyone else was out here, braving the high-noon heat and the late-night drops with only their sleeping bags, tying their bod-ies to trunks, fighting for something bigger than themselves. He wanted to be part of this.

But maybe one day. He'd call his mom back in the morning, if the service held up.

As he tucked his phone into his pocket, he looked out over the woods. The bark on the trees glowed red with the setting sun. He heard the tinny sounds of a guitar traveling up from the campsite. Noa was serenading the others with an acoustic version of "'03 Bonnie & Clyde." Xavier's stomach twisted. He missed Mar so badly it hurt.

Suddenly, a few feet away on a neighboring branch, Xavier saw two beady, pitch-black eyes staring at him. The creature's brown coat was painted with small strokes of white, its feathers arching out from its eyes in two dramatic, inquisitive brows. A spotted owl.

The majestic bird shifted from one foot to the other, settling into its spot. It hooted, a single low exhalation, expanding and contracting the air around it. A shiver ran down Xavier's spine.

Quietly, a little bit embarrassed, Xavier hooted back. The bird padded again from foot to foot. It cried out, almost playfully. Xavier laughed. At first cautiously, then full-throatedly, he howled.

———

Some two hundred miles south, past the cliffs that jutted out over the Mendocino coast, beyond the wind-swept dunes of Bodega Bay, inland from the endangered snowy plovers laying eggs in the protected sands of Point Reyes, deep in the woods of Claremont Canyon, an old power line swung in the wind.

The national weather service predicted high heat throughout the Bay over the coming days, warned of possible seventy-mile-per-hour winds—conditions ripe for fire.

Just to the east of Berkeley, at the crossroads where the asphalt of Panoramic Way met the dry, cracked earth of Stonewall Trail, the twisted cables swayed. The electric company had that very intersection listed somewhere far down in a document keeping track of outdated lines overdue for maintenance.

As night fell over the city, a strong gust of wind blew through, sending house lights flickering. People seated at dinner looked at each other, startled, then burst out in an uneasy laughter. Some cursed at the TV that cut out just as the game was getting good. Others still didn't notice at all, having taken advantage of the unusually warm fall night to go for a stroll in search of ice cream.

At the edge of the woods, the line snapped. Its black cord whipped about, fizzling at one end, sending showers of bright light into the darkness. A tiny spark flew from its lips, landing at the foot of a hundred-year-old pine. There, on the forest floor, it crackled in the dark.

ACKNOWLEDGMENTS

To my book team: my agent, Sharon Pelletier, whose advocacy and enthu-siasm buoy me on this uncertain journey and whose advice I trust completely; to my editor, David Howe, whose generous and incisive edits made this book infinitely better; to everyone at Harper: Janet Rosenberg for her diligent copyedits, Alicia Gencarelli for her fantastic production editing, Allison Hargraves for her eagle-eyed proofreading, Elina Cohen for her interior design, Joanne O'Neill for the stunning cover, and everyone in publicity and marketing who helped usher this book into readers' hands—thank you. Solidarity, always, with the HarperCollins union.

To my high school English teacher Mrs. Reilly: it was in your classroom that I fell in love with books, and with your faith in me that I believed that one day I could write one.

To the authors whose books I turned to as I wrote this novel, for comfort and transcendence, whose shoulders I humbly stand on, to name just a few: Brit Bennett, Ross Gay, Yaa Gyasi, Anne Lamott, Min Jin Lee, Ada Limón, Celeste Ng, Jenny Odell.

To my early readers, to whom I am forever indebted: Dara, Chloé, Miche, Meya, Camille, Clémentine, Laurence, Joyce, Dad, Sisi, Maman, Rick, Caro, Emma, Ellie, Loreto, Vicky, Randy, Helen, Derwin, Dan, Seans. Your edits and encouragement are etched into every page.

To Randy and our group: I am so grateful for us. You changed my life so profoundly; nothing that I do, or that I am, would be without you.

Para Claudia, gracias por cuidar tan bien a nuestro hogar—tu trabajo es de lo más esencial; y Ariana y Esme, gracias por amar tanto a nuestro perrito y ser dos corazones tan grandes. También agradezco a Gloria Elizabeth Hidalgo, que me crió con tanto amor.

To mes copines: Joyce, my bubu; Cam, my floser; Lau, mon petit coeur; Clem, mon chou; Emma, mon âm(m)e; and Meya, my BFF, Tweedledee to my Tweedledum, my forever person. You are my family.

To my sisterfriends: Dara, my first reader and treasured twin; Rachie, for your gift of *The Artist's Way*; Miche, who showed me how to live your art; Alysha, who writes to heal; et Chloé, mon amour, c'est le miracle de ma vie de t'avoir trouvée.

To my parents: Maman, who read with me in bed every night; Dad, who is my favorite storyteller (and spiel giver); Sisi, who gifted me Virginia Woolf and taught me that women's stories matter; and Rick, who was my biggest fan before my books were ever published—because of you, I grew up feeling unconditionally loved. Thank you for being my biggest supporters and best examples of how to live a generous life.

To my siblings: Jadi and Dodo—thank you for being my first buddies, my fiercest board-game foes. I love you.

To my niblings: River, Tommy, Palo y Rafa, Ben and Norah—being your Titi is my favorite thing.

To the matriarchs of our family: Mazon and Grandma, two fervent lovers of books.

And, finally, to Adri, mi vida, mi media naranja. Te adoro. Thank you for how you make me laugh and how you help me breathe. For your boundless love and support. Y por ser tú mismo. Je t'aime pour le reste de ma vie.

ABOUT THE AUTHOR

SARAH RUIZ-GROSSMAN is a writer and former reporter at *Huff-Post*, where she covered the climate crisis and other social justice issues. She lives in California with her husband and their pit bull.